Jesus wants me for a **sunbeam**

Jesus wants me for a sunbeam

PETER GOLDSWORTHY

A novella with extensive reading notes

flamingo
An imprint of HarperCollins*Publishers*

Flamingo
An imprint of HarperCollins*Publishers*

'Jesus Wants Me For A Sunbeam' was first published in 1993
in *Little Deaths*, HarperCollins
This edition first published in 1999
by HarperCollins*Publishers* Pty Limited
ACN 009 913 517
A member of the HarperCollins*Publishers* (Australia) Pty Limited Group
http://www.harpercollins.com.au

Copyright © Peter Goldsworthy 1993
Revised and extended 1999
The essay 'Death and the Comedian' was published
in *Navel Gazing*, Penguin, 1998

This book is copyright.
Apart from any fair dealing for the purposes of private study, research,
criticism or review, as permitted under the Copyright Act, no part may be
reproduced by any process without written permission.
Inquiries should be addressed to the publishers.

Every effort has been made to trace copyright holders of material quoted
herein. In cases where this has been unsuccessful, please address any
inquiries to the publishers.

HarperCollins*Publishers*
25 Ryde Road, Pymble, Sydney, NSW 2073, Australia
31 View Road, Glenfield, Auckland 10, New Zealand
77–85 Fulham Palace Road, London, W6 8JB, United Kingdom
Hazelton Lanes, 55 Avenue Road, Suite 2900, Toronto, Ontario M5R 3L2
and 1995 Markham Road, Scarborough, Ontario M1B 5M8, Canada
10 East 53rd Street, New York NY 10022, USA

National Library of Australia Cataloguing-in-Publication data:

Goldsworthy, Peter, 1951- .
Jesus wants me for a sunbeam.
ISBN 0 7322 6745 5
I. Title.
A823.3

Cover image/photograph by Kate Mitchell
Printed in Australia by Griffin Press Pty Ltd Adelaide,
on 79gsm Bulky Paperback

5 4 3 2 1   99 00 01 02

CONTENTS

Introduction by Amanda Lohrey   1

Jesus Wants Me For A Sunbeam   11

Reading Notes: 85

   Afterword   87

   Poetry   92

   Essay   101

   Reviews   114

   About Peter Goldsworthy   125

   Discussion Questions   129

INTRODUCTION

The reader might begin to browse through this volume and discover that the novella at its centre is very short and has been published before. The question might then come to mind: why publish it anew? The answer to that is simple: *Jesus Wants Me For A Sunbeam* is one of the best things written in Australia in the modern era – it would not be too strong to call it a masterpiece. When first published in 1993 as one in the collection of stories, *Little Deaths*, the quality of the work was immediately recognised by perceptive critics like Andrew Riemer and hailed as a *tour de force*, but collections of short stories are not as popular in the market as they once were and many readers, even admirers of Goldsworthy's earlier work, remain unaware of the fact that a brilliant gem lay buried in an otherwise unexceptional volume.

The novella has long been the Cinderella form of Australian letters and *Jesus Wants Me For A Sunbeam* demonstrates just how much it can be made to do in the hands of a maestro. Although *Sunbeam* runs to no more than 14 250 words it has the dramatic intensity and thematic richness of a much longer work. It also does that very difficult and rare thing in fiction which is to create a convincing portrait of a good man. The young lovers at its centre, Richard and Linda, are exemplary offspring of the white Protestant middle-class, as nice a young couple as the leafy suburbs of Adelaide can nurture. '*Solid, nice, good: these were the specifications of their world.*' Sweethearts since their student days they do everything together in a blissful symbiotic cocoon which, for all that, is not entirely complacent. They know there is suffering out there and they do their best to make the right gestures – sponsoring a child in Bangladesh – but for the most part theirs is a life that knows no disturbance other than the horrors of the nightly news. To this they respond, characteristically, by disposing of their television set, and spending the evenings reading aloud to one another from the classics.

Into this ordered affectionate world they bring their own two children; first, Ben, and three years later, Emma. In their own minds the ideal of themselves as sensible and virtuous is further confirmed by the perfect symmetry of this reproduction. A boy and girl at first try: it seems a just reward, *'if their good fortune was not exactly planned, it was, she felt, at least deserved. It was earnt'* and their son's smile *'seemed to bestow on them God's personal, unspoken benediction'*. But despite this Protestant sense of the Elect, intimations of mortality persist in haunting the margins of their lives. Linda especially is resistant to these and finds herself, after the birth of her daughter, unable any longer to go to the movies, *'disturbed, she explained, by their increasing violence'*. Another door is closed on the world as the young couple strive to protect themselves from misery and death. Here is a portrait of family life as control, order, exclusion; of the suburban ideal as a first line of defence against pain.

When things go wrong for the charmed young couple their instinctive response is to look for a rational explanation of cause and effect. Theirs is the modern mind, resistant in every way to the idea of blind Fate or Divine Will. Though churchgoers (an interesting detail on Goldsworthy's part) their faith is thin. It's an habitual – one might even say, social – religious observance rather than true spiritual passion, and when placed under stress it evaporates. The clergyman who comes to console them is shown to the door, and Rick announces that from now on they will have to rely on themselves. In this sense *Sunbeam* is a portrait of the secular mind at its heart's centre – stripped of any of the great master narratives that confer meaning on life (such as the Christian notion of Redemption) the family has only itself to fall back on, hence the touching depiction of the family room (that ubiquitous legacy to domestic architecture from the Seventies) as a kind of shrine: '. . . *it occurred to Rick that this room had always been their true place of worship, not Church – and that these three people, his family, his ideal of Family, had always been the core of whatever he believed in.*'

Peter Goldsworthy has long been our pre-eminent poet of suburbia, of its ethical and metaphysical terrain, and *Sunbeam* is a moving meditation on the terrifying abyss that lies beneath the decent and the ordinary. In the thirteen sections that make up the novella Goldsworthy sets out with almost clinical spareness an unbearably affecting portrait of a father's love for his child, and at the same time the spiritual desolation behind it. In the most mundane of suburban settings he gives us a story of madness and heroism, not on any epic stage – on the battlefield, or the streets – but in the most ordinary of homes. He does this by taking a common idea – that our children are a part of us, and we of them, and extending that idea to its most extreme point. I can think of no other work in literature that so powerfully reflects on what it means to be a parent; to love a child and to be, in every sense, responsible for that child. Where does that responsibility end? What do we mean when we say that we 'love' our children? What are the boundaries of that love? Its breaking point? What is the role – if any – of Reason in arriving at answers to these questions? Is love beyond the rational? Ultimately Rick comes to a decision to protect his daughter in a way that is both quite rational and yet utterly insane. How can it be both at once?

Throughout the novella there is a great play on the question of what is and isn't reasonable. How far can the human *cogito* take us? What has it given us that we can fall back on in the moment of our extremity? Can it save us? This is the great Enlightenment project, stripped of all spiritual authority and it has been one of the seminal themes of Goldsworthy's *oeuvre*. Science and Reason were meant to compensate for the loss of divine redemption but Science, as Goldsworthy demonstrates in his fiction elsewhere (*Honk If You Are Jesus*, *Wish*) is all too fallible. It merely generates ever new and mutating moral dilemmas to which Reason can offer only a series of free-floating rationalisations. One of the most remarkable things about *Sunbeam* is the way it takes these grand themes and scales them down to a suburban setting without any affectation or straining after effect. Consider the way in which even that epicentre of Enlightenment rationalism at its most extreme – the French Revolution – is effortlessly absorbed into the texture of the narrative, simply and poetically echoed in Rick and Linda's reading of Dickens' *A Tale of Two Cities*, and Rick's ongoing image of his daughter as a prisoner in tumbrils.

More than any other Australian writer I can think of, Peter Goldsworthy is absorbed in the now, a conscientious chronicler of his age and generation. Like those other writers who were doctors, Chekhov and (for a time) Maugham he is not much interested in archetypal romances and mysteries and still less in mythopoeic histories. From a daily practice of looking at the wound(s) up close he seeks to make sense of the way we live now, to explore the meaning of the contemporary moment. And it seems to me that *Sunbeam* is a story that only a baby-boomer could have written. The post-war generation grew up in the most prosperous and optimistic period of this century, and the most secular, in which affluence guaranteed freedom from hunger and gave rise to a naive faith in science and technology which included the promise of a cure for all our ills. Population growth meant new suburbs where increasingly the nuclear family became the intense focus of everything and the untidy, asymmetrical groupings of the extended family a thing of the past, at least in the white Anglo household. Added to all this, the women's movement of the 60s and 70s helped to create a generation of men who believed in more involved fathering. Steven Spielberg's radical rewriting of the Peter Pan story in his movie *Hook* is really about the baby-boomers coming to believe that there is no greater imperative in their mature adult lives than the psychological nurturing of their children – which is not to say that earlier generations didn't love theirs, but fathers then were harder pressed to put food on the table. They had more children to spread their affections around and they had less expectation of immunity from modern medicine. I think it can be argued that now, more than any other time in history, the child is the projection of the utopian secular Self, and the agnostic's only claim to immortality. A lot is at stake. Goldsworthy doesn't judge this, he simply holds up a mirror to our own obsessionality, and then takes it one step further.

That so much in this short novella is achieved in so few words is one of the marvels of its form. Goldsworthy's style has a clarity and simplicity – one could even say, humility – as if it came to the reader direct from the gods with the writer there as mere conduit of some special grace. This of course is an illusion the writer has worked hard to create. In reality such a style requires immense discipline, not to mention acute timing (the way a crucial word is dropped into the narrative in such a way as to fall like a hammer on the reader's heart). In its self-effacing control it can be compared to the regularity of the heartbeat – one false word, one awkward rhythm in the phrasing and the mesmeric spell of the narrative, the sense of inescapable Fate, is broken. Paradoxically, it's a kind of writing that gains its distinctive strength from the fact that while it must rely on words to come into being it has at the same time a very great distrust of them. Not the least of *Sunbeam*'s riches is that it can be read as a meditation upon textuality itself, upon the word and its powerful role in western civilisation as a source of meaning and consolation. During the middle stages of their ordeal the young couple, Rick and Linda, read aloud to one another from *A Tale of Two Cities*. '*It's a far better thing I do than I have ever done; it is a far, far better rest I go to than*

I have ever had.' At first they find this fortifying, for here in the heroism of romantic literature is a marvellous echoing of their own dilemma. But ultimately even their beloved books fail them. Too many dead children. *'A volume of Dickens lay discarded on the floor; another waif had died; he had become unreadable.'* Still, in the final moments before the denouement the young parents resort once again to the consolations of reading, this time the Bible. *'Yea, though I walk through the valley of the shadow of death, I will fear no evil: for thou art with me . . .'* Though Rick is sceptical, something in the very vibration of the words, in their music, affects him. *'. . . he might believe in little beyond family love, but these words seemed the culmination of all their nights of book-readings, as if those thick books — Dickens, George Eliot, Thackeray — had been a preparation for this moment, this last distillation of the written word.'*

What is this mysterious distillation of the written word that the book offers us? What is the meaning – in the Biblical sense – of The Word in our culture? Why write? Why read? Why would a doctor set aside his 'useful' work to spend hours re-arranging words on a page? Is it all just so much blather and distraction or can books make a difference – this is an argument that the writer goes on having with himself, from year to year, and book to book. And while it may sound at first like a somewhat self-referential project, the very best books are the ones that succeed, through the alchemy of storytelling, in offering that argument to the reader as a form of the sublime. In so doing they draw the reader into their world with such profound intuitive artistry that the process of reading itself becomes an act of communion. It's a rare book that can accomplish all this, and *Jesus Wants Me For A Sunbeam* is one of them.

AMANDA LOHREY 1999

Jesus wants me for a **sunbeam**

'In us we trust.' JOHN BERRYMAN

1.

Richard and Linda. Benjamin and Emma. To outsiders, the Pollards seemed more a single indivisible organism than four separate members of a family: a symmetrical unit.

Examined from any angle that unit presented the same number of faces to the world: mirror faces, crystal facets. Two adults, two children. Two females, two males. A father, a mother. A son, a daughter.

Simple statistics, perhaps – unimportant, even trivial, in themselves – but to Rick and Linda, in love with each other and in love with their children, they were an emblem of something larger: of the balance and self-sufficiency of their lives. It seemed to the young parents that not much else was needed, that *any*thing else – a third child, a live-in grandmother, a dog, a cat, even a pet-rock – would be somehow excessive, and unbalancing.

'One of each,' friends remarked, enviously, after the birth of their second. 'You're so *lucky*.'

Linda always feigned chagrin at this: 'Credit where credit's due – it took years of careful planning.'

She was not entirely joking. If their good fortune was not exactly planned, it was, she felt, at least deserved. It was earnt.

More symmetries emerged as the years passed, equally unplanned – or at most half-planned. Often these were merely whimsical: that both adults were Capricorns, both children Sagittarians. Other symmetries seemed more significant, and meaningful. And even useful: that father and daughter were left-handers, mother and son orthodox, would surely make for exciting family doubles on the tennis court in future years.

The more such symmetries came to light, the more both parents actively sought them out. It became a family game, from which data that didn't fit were excluded, or conveniently ignored: that both children had been dealt their father's mud-brown eyes, for instance.

Their mother's were blue: a pale sky-blue.

Rick and Linda had been happy themselves as children, sheltered in the leafier avenues of the city. Both came from solid families, grew up in nice areas, attended good schools. Solid, nice, good: these were the specifications of their world, interchangeable, universally applicable. They had first met at a suburban Public Library, as teenagers, studying for final school exams, and felt their way cautiously into love. Their discovery of sex had come, equally cautiously, through each other, and only through each other: a slow, almost courtly process of escalating excitements spread over many months. Even after several dozen of those months, Linda would still involuntarily cover her face with her hands at the moment of greatest pleasure, as if shamed by that pleasure, and its sign: the crimson flush that spread across her cheeks and neck.

They had married while still at University. It seemed a precipitate step, the first missed beat in a measured rhythm. Both sets of parents were agreed on this – but the young couple, pimple-spotted, barely beyond their teens, had smiled their way past any objections. Strengthened by each other, they had grown immune to parental advice – they could, they found, outlast it. Their constant physical contact – twined fingers, pressed thighs, stolen kisses – seemed to fuse them ever more closely together, amoeba-like, doubling their intelligence and resolve. Both now knew that they were halves of something larger, that their lives before – their 'previous lives', Rick joked – had been incomplete.

They had married in St Paul's, Linda's parish church. They chose the recently arrived Father Cummings as celebrant — a young student-priest, or priest-intern whom Linda had met through the church Youth Group — rather than the older rector whom her parents preferred. John Cummings was their own age; he had permitted a revised set of vows in which both partners promised to love, honour and cherish, but from which the ancient asymmetrical duty of wifely obedience had been removed.

The young couple had salvaged a few dusty, spidery pieces of furniture from the cellars and attics and backsheds of their reluctant families, and rented a small student-flat in the inner-city suburbs. To the two families it seemed that their children were still playing at being grown-ups, that this tiny, cramped flat was not far removed from the dolls' houses and backyard cubbies of a few years before. Both sets of parents offered the support of weekly meals, and a monthly allowance. 'Pocket-money' was the term the two fathers preferred, as if the words might somehow preserve a child-like dependency. At times, as if bidding against each other in an auction of allegiance, the two mothers offered help with house-cleaning and laundry.

'You won't have *time* with all your studies, dear,' Rick's mother urged her new daughter-in-law. 'Why don't I pick up a laundry basket each week?'

'Rick does the laundry, Mother,' Linda said, a little smugly. 'You'll have to speak to him.'

The older woman was incredulous: '*Rick* does the laundry? But he's never washed a thing in his life.'

'He's a quick learner.'

'But the breadwinner *especially* has to study.'

To Rick and Linda it was the beginning of a shared, equal adventure. Snuggling together each night, it seemed a crime that both had been forced to sleep all those years apart, alone, in a narrow child's bed. It might have been something out of Dickens, Linda joked: a cruelty that happened to orphans. Each evening after lectures they took long walks together through their new neighbourhood, holding hands, and at home afterwards shared a steaming, brimming bath. After making love, they often read passages to each other from their favourite books, which were, increasingly, the same books. Over breakfast they chose items from the morning paper which they also read aloud, as if feeding each other handpicked delicacies. They packed frugal student-lunches which they ate together on the library lawns between lectures. Each Saturday they played mixed doubles in the local lawn-court Club competition, each Sunday they pedalled their push-bikes — their old school-bikes, resurrected on the cheap — long-distance, visiting families and friends. Their physical resemblance to each other — near-identical height and body-build — seemed to become more pronounced through those first years of marriage, as if eating the same food, and sharing the same exercise caused an even closer convergence of body-types. Without exactly planning it, Rick permitted his hair to grow a little longer, Linda cropped hers shorter; they chose, independently, similar gold-rimmed glasses. They often wore each other's T-shirts, and even, at a stretch, before the birth of Ben, each other's jeans.

Their shoe-sizes alone refused to converge, although lying together in bed — naked, limb-entwined — they would occasionally compare their four bare feet, and pretend, playfully, that there had been some shrinkage or enlargement.

'Is that your foot or mine?'

'Wriggle your toes.'

'It must be mine — but it doesn't *look* like mine. Is it my right foot or my left foot?'

'Perhaps you should have them tattooed.'

'Left and Right?'

'Love and Hate — like bikies have engraved on their fists.'

'Which foot is the love foot?'

'Let's find out.'

After the initial hesitations and shames, their bodies had become sources of astonishment, companions on a nightly descent into the deepest trenches of pleasure. Two years of such bliss followed the wedding — the years before the birth of Ben, their first child — but when they looked back on those two years later, their lives still seemed to be lacking something. Even the memories of those early days of awkward, thrilled sexual discovery faded, even the milestone of their graduation from university, and their first appointments as teachers in the same suburban high school seemed to belong to a previous life: Life Before Ben.

The birth was premature, the labour difficult, the baby undersize. Afterwards, Rick sat on the edge of his wife's bed, holding the tiny, scrawny bundle with great care.

'He's very beautiful,' he said, 'for a frog.'

Linda clutched at her sore belly, groaning with joy: 'Don't make me laugh, *please.*'

The baby refused to sleep. He sniffled and wheezed. He regurgitated more food than he ate, but still filled an endless procession of nappies, refuting all known laws of the conservation of matter. And, always — and even more always at night — he cried. He *screamed*. To Rick and Linda, still surprised to find themselves parents, energised by astonishment and excitement, these trials seemed no more than rites of passage, small sufferings that were more ritualised pleasure than pain: trials half-dreaded but also half-hoped for, expected, *imagined*, and therefore surmountable. Once again there was no end of outside help: both pairs of grandparents competed with offers of daily child-minding. Linda's mother, a volunteer worker for Meals-on-Wheels, once even dropped off a spare meal for the young couple, driving miles out of her weekly round among the pensioners and disabled.

'Leftovers from the kitchen,' she explained, defending this small corruption. 'We would only have thrown it out.'

It was thrown out, after she had left, behind her back. The thought counted, Linda declared, even if the food was inedible.

The world that surrounded the young family seemed charmed; every face that turned towards them was smiling, wishing them well, offering help. Their neighbours — Greeks, mostly, in their inner-city suburb – showered them with baby-gifts, and honey-cakes, and pastries drenched with icing-sugar, and incomprehensible advice.

'He's so ugly!' one black-clad widow peered into the stroller and declared, loudly, to persuade the Evil Eye the baby was not worth troubling with, and the phrase soon became a refrain, and then, after a month or two, a pet-name.

'Your turn to bath Ugly.'

'Ugly needs his nappy changed.'

At school, their fellow teachers were benignly tolerant of late arrivals and missed classes. Even the occasional hurried escape from a Church sermon with a howling baby on Sundays was warmed by the glow of a hundred older and more knowledgeable faces – and a pause and patient smile from young Reverend Cummings high in the pulpit.

His boyish, slightly podgy smile seemed to bestow on them God's personal, unspoken benediction.

2.

Their world was charmed and protected, but not ignorant: news from beyond the municipal limits filtered through. That the lives of others might not be so charmed was clear to them, at least in abstract. Their imaginations did not fail them. They dropped generous donations into the Church Christmas Bowl and Easter Appeal each year; they fostered a World Care child in Bangladesh after the birth of Ben, and after Emma's birth three years later, fostered another in Ecuador.

Once a year a Christmas card and letter arrived from each child, written with obsessive neatness in Spanish, or the weird extra-terrestrial script of Bengali. Typed, misspelt English translations always accompanied both haiku-sized letters, their tones identically flat and formulaic despite their separate origins, as if written by the same child, or the same computer. Snapshots were sometimes clipped to the letters, and perhaps these were also of the same child: a small hollow-eyed waif, dressed in ill-fitting Best Clothes, probably an older sibling's, posed in front of a squalid shanty, half Kim, half Oliver Twist.

They decided not to answer these letters. It seemed demeaning, even humiliating to compel a child to write thankyou letters, to report annually to its benefactors — to beg, in essence. They sought no gratitude. Nor did they seek knowledge. Their quarterly donation was offered up to *prevent* misery, not to learn about it. The payments were debited, automatically, invisibly, against their joint bank account.

'We do more than most,' Linda argued. 'We shouldn't have to wear a hairshirt as well.'

'You don't think we're sticking our heads in the sand?'

'I can't see the point in torturing ourselves with details. It won't change anything.'

After the birth of Emma she refused, suddenly, to go to the movies for similar reasons – disturbed, she explained, by their increasing violence. The announcement, again, caused only token argument from her husband – their minds, moving in tandem on most issues, had converged again on this. She had merely put their joint thought into words.

The thought was waiting to be spoken by one of them, its final choice of mouth was unimportant.

To some extent the film-boycott was academic: their two infant children permitted little time for movie-going. Ben reverted to his earlier, more demanding state with the birth of his sister: waking at night, refusing food, vomiting at will whenever the baby received too much attention. House-moving added another upheaval to his life. They had outgrown their narrow student-house; now, with help from the four grandparents – a loan for the deposit – they took out a mortgage on a small villa a little further from the city, and a little closer to the golden suburbs of their childhood.

Linda's boycott of the television news a few months after house-moving was not so academic. The decision was reached, or cemented into words, on a late summer Sunday evening. The young couple had arrived home after a long day of tennis, tucked tired children into early beds – *trapped* them in bed, bound beneath tight sheets – and settled themselves in the television nook with chopsticks and shallow silverfoil trays of Chinese take-away. Was their mood too tranquil, too pleasantly weary, too resistant to any disturbance? The lead-story on the news was surely no more horrific, or blood-spattered, than usual, but Linda shivered – suddenly, involuntarily – and averted her eyes from the screen.

'How horrible,' she said, and turned to her husband. 'Turn it off. Please.'

He hesitated, momentarily: the evening news was a ritual he enjoyed, a warm shower at the end of the day. Its actual content was somehow less important than the comfort of the form: a cathode-ray squirt of images, a steady horizontal stream that washed through his tired mind, beaming him up and away to other places in the world, places so far removed from his world that they might have been other planets. As he wavered, Linda seized the remote control and waved it at the screen; a talking head contracted to a bright pinhead, then vanished, a smooth-shaven genie sucked back inside its bottle.

'Why do they *show* things like that?'

For once he felt the stirring of real argument: 'Because it happens, sweetheart.'

'Why can't they show good news for a change? The million *good* things people do every day? They always choose the one bad thing.'

'Perhaps we should try to understand it.'

'How can you *understand* it? A man who murders his entire family, then himself!'

She shivered again, as disturbed by her own blunt summary of events as she had been by the original story.

'Maybe he did it out of love,' Rick suggested, weirdly.

She stared at him, incredulous: '*What?*'

He watched the blank screen as if waiting for more information, trying to understand this odd germ of a thought, to *grow* it.

'Misplaced love,' he said, groping. 'If you're depressed, and the world is not worth living in, you want to save your loved ones from it. You want to protect them.'

He paused, caught her astonished eye, and added, hastily: 'Maybe.'

They sat in silence, stunned: Rick even more than his wife, mystified by the origins of these words that had jumped from his mouth, unpremeditated. With his chopsticks he poked a wad of rice into that mouth, and chewed, allowing himself a little thinking time.

Linda saved him from further inspirations; she came up with a more convincing theory: 'I think it's merely selfish. They want someone to go *with* them.'

Rick swallowed his food. 'Like the Egyptian pharaohs,' he said, 'taking their whole households into the pyramids, buried alive.'

Their thoughts were back in harmony.

'Or the rajahs in India,' she said, remembering a movie she had seen as a child, 'burning their wives on their own funeral pyres.'

She shuddered, then jerked up out of her chair as if disguising the shudder in a larger, more deliberate movement. Finding herself on her feet, she moved down the hall, and softly, protectively, closed the doors to the bedrooms where the children slept.

'This is morbid,' she whispered as she returned. 'How did we get onto this?'

'The news.'

'Let's talk about something else.'

Her husband resisted one last time; still tantalised, perhaps, by his earlier heresy: 'I know it's unpleasant, but should we turn our backs on the world?'

'If we can't change it, what's the point? I don't want to *know* about those ugly things. I don't see why I should have to.'

She watched him, waiting for agreement.

'We do what we can,' she repeated. 'We do our bit. Why should we thrust our noses in it?'

She was right, he knew. You had to draw chalklines, erect barricades. There was so much pain and misery in the world you would drown in it: a great ocean of pain, of which the cathode-ray tube sprayed only a few selected drops in their direction each night. With the zeal of a convert, or of a fresh runner in a relay, he took the argument from her and carried it further:

'Maybe we should sell the television. Or give it away. Get rid of it altogether. Especially with the children getting older.'

They watched each other for a few further seconds. At length Rick rose, and wedged open the back door.

Without a word he unplugged the television set, carried it outside and heaved it into the backseat of his car. A theatrical gesture, perhaps — the disgraced television would sit there for several days, tamely buckled in a rear seat-belt, before being traded in for a new sound-system — but both felt somehow cleaner, even purified: a satisfaction akin to the sweet aftermath of spring-cleaning.

New routines quickly replaced the old. Their evenings were filled with music, with educational games — Scrabble, crosswords, Trivial Pursuit — and, once again, with books.

The young couple had inherited a reverence for books. Both had brought several tea-chests packed with books to the marriage: an intellectual dowry of children's books, old school texts, gift-sets of Shakespeare and Shaw and Jane Austen and assorted Brontës, plus, from Linda's side, everything that Dickens had ever written: a metre-length, at least, of matching volumes, bound in calf, plus assorted dog-eared school-paperback editions of the same. These had multiplied in the years since: each Christmas they received as gifts almost as many books as they gave. Their shelves — makeshift constructions of plank and brick — were crammed: unread books, many of them, but their presence alone was reassuring, their names were a kind of incantation, like the names of saints or household gods: small geometric household gods of learning and self-improvement and uplift; protectors against ignorance. The books had worn more sacred with time. They were dipped into, like the Bible, as sources of quotations, and poetry, and Trivial Pursuit clues – but seldom read.

Until now. Delivered from television, Linda decided they should read aloud to each other every night, as they had in the first days of marriage, before children.

'And as my father read to me,' she announced over a meal one night, and immediately rose and began tugging books from the shelves before turning to invite Rick to help, or even to agree.

'Where shall we start?' she wondered aloud.

'Anywhere but Dickens,' he said, teasing.

She smiled, and squeezed the calf-bound book she had already selected back into a narrow slot among its fellows, and tugged out a slim paperback.

'I taught that last year,' he protested.

'Then you can read it to me.'

'I'd prefer something with more meat.'

'You mean more fat,' she said, but returned the book to the shelf, before selecting something thicker.

At first there were frequent interruptions. Emma, placid from birth, slept unbroken from early evening to early morning — but her older brother insisted on staying awake with his parents. The television had often kept him tranquillised in the past, now new routines were needed. A war of attrition followed — a war of tears and nerve and bluff — ending in the parents' capitulation. Weary of running to the child's bedroom every few minutes, it simply seemed easier to have him with them, playing on the rug in the lounge, late at night. Listening to, or at least hearing, their book-readings also had a soothing, hypnotic effect on the child. His eyes soon drooped shut, his restless twitching ceased — often, oddly, at the end of a chapter, or on the last page of a book, as if cued by some subtle change in the tone of his mother's voice. Or was it some resolution in the music of the words themselves, words whose meanings were still largely beyond him?

'*The growing good of the world,*' Linda recited, '*is partly dependant on unhistoric acts; and that things are not so ill with you and me as they might have been, is half-owing to the number who have lived faithfully a hidden life, and rest in unvisited tombs.*'

Rick — if he was still awake — would rise and carry the sleeping boy to bed at the end of such passages; this was the sign for a general lights-out.

Isolated from the wider world, their small life contracted even more tightly about their children, their family board-games and book-readings. Old friends from University, staff-room colleagues from school — many still single — were rarely seen. There seemed so little time. Linda had chosen to stay at home with Ben for the first year; Rick took leave without pay the following year while she returned to work. The opposite pattern continued with the birth of Emma. Rick spent the year at home, mothering her; Linda went back to school.

'But what of Rick's career?' his mother summoned the courage to inquire one evening as she collected their weekly laundry.

'The family is my career, Mum.'

Linda added: 'In ten years everyone will share work like this, Mother.'

The young couple exchanged satisfied smiles behind the older woman's back. They felt themselves to be pioneers, ahead of their time, and relished their notoriety among less 'liberated' friends. That Rick's mother still did the family's laundry, and Linda's mother still bestowed a weekly meal, went unacknowledged. The mothers wanted to help; Rick appreciated the extra time this permitted him to spend with his adored baby daughter. Emma was a small serious child: slow and methodical in her movements, a watcher of games rather than a participant. Her nickname – 'Wol' – came from Rick, amused by his daughter's solemn owl-like appearance, wise beyond her years.

With Ben at kindergarten now for much of each day, Rick's life revolved around his daughter: reading stories, reciting rhymes, singing songs, playing games, fingerpainting, visiting local playgrounds and paddling pools – and each Wednesday taking her to the neighbourhood play-group, sole father among a gathering of mildly discomfited mothers.

'It seemed a little . . . awkward,' he reported home to Linda after the first. 'Long silences.'

'They'll get used to you.'

He sat through the weekly coffee and carrot-cake and largely ignored the gossip that soon began to fill the silences. The women might not have been there, he had eyes and ears only for his precious Wol, studying her interactions with other children, protecting her against their viciousness, excusing her own as over-tiredness – and memorising every detail to report back later to Linda. And so within their family geometry a further symmetry, or mirror-reflection, was growing: the father was closer to the daughter, the mother to the son.

3.

Emma's sore throat seemed trivial at first: another of the shared communal viruses that were swapped back and forth between the toddlers at play-group like counters, or dice, in a board-game. Ben, at school now, also brought home a regular supply of sniffly noses and sore throats to share with her. He had always been the sickly one; missing one or two days a fortnight of school, his alleged ugliness failing to ward off the invisible influence of germs. Emma seemed made of tougher gristle — less complaining, more robust. Rick and Linda paid little attention to her symptoms at first.

But the swollen glands remained swollen; a blood screen hinted at vague abnormalities.

Their local doctor — silver-haired, silver-tongued — was reassuring as he studied the print-out.

'I've seen numbers like this before,' he said. 'No cause for concern. Probably just a virus.'

'Could it be serious?'

He shook his head: 'Of course we'll repeat the test in a week or two. Just to make sure everything is back to normal.'

Rick and Linda exchanged glances: 'Then it *could* be serious?'

He smiled reassuringly, but the smile seemed to lack something: 'I can't see any point in worrying about it yet.'

They worried for a week: in small bursts at first, but lengthening, and growing uncontrollably as the child failed to improve.

The repeat screen was equally ambiguous. The doctor, while conceding the figures on his print-out 'might' not be as normal as he had first thought, still refused to name any disease, or even nominate a short-list of candidates. He filibustered smoothly for some time before Linda interrupted:

'If it might be something, *what* might it be?'

'It would be premature to say. There are many possibilities.'

'Serious?'

'Some serious, some not so serious. But that applies to any illness . . . '

Rick and Linda rose simultaneously, angrily; Rick demanded a copy of both test print-outs which were reluctantly provided. From the receptionist's phone they made an urgent call, and drove immediately to the rooms of a specialist paediatrician: Eve Harrison, an old school friend of Linda's. Short, compact, quick-talking, Eve had been known for her frankness at school; she showed no hesitation in applying a label to the blood screens at first glance, a word Rick and Linda had already begun to sense, if only from the glare of its previous absence.

Like most parents, they had rehearsed over the years for that moment, emotionally: the moment they might hear the word leukaemia spoken to *them*, spoken *at* them. They had read the true stories, had tears jerked from them by films based on real-life events. They had grieved, vicariously, for other children: small strangers who were nevertheless part of the shared public property of parenthood. News of the illnesses of these others — friends of cousins of friends, or cousins of friends of cousins — spread as rapidly as jokes or gossip through a vast network of waiting, eavesdropping parents, in hushed, horrified tones.

'*Such* a lovely family.'

'Nothing can be done? Surely *these* days — with all the new drugs . . . '

Beneath the horror of such stories there was also, surely, a deeper half-hidden note of relief: that it wasn't happening to them, and theirs. Perhaps there was even an odd warped gratitude towards the victim, who had somehow — although this dark thought would never be put into words — saved everyone else by being chosen in their place: a statistical scape-goat, a statistical sacrifice.

For Rick and Linda there was also, at the end of that terrible week of waiting and worry, an odd feeling of relief that it *had* happened to them, and theirs. Anything was better than uncertainty; the waiting had been intolerable, the fear of the unmentionable had almost come to be a desire for the unmentionable; its certainty, its *mention*, was at least a resolution. To finally hear the word spoken aloud provided a focus for worry, a definite enemy that they could now face, and fight, together, as a family.

A bone marrow biopsy the following morning gave an even clearer view of this enemy.

'Remission is possible,' Eve Harrison told them. 'But everyone who has this type dies of it, eventually.'

The young parents glanced at each other, more composed and prepared: 'How long?'

'The mean survival rate is three years. Fifty per cent of the victims are still alive at three years.'

They felt almost grateful again for these blunt figures: three years was better than, say, three months. They felt, after the initial diagnosis had taken everything away, that they had been given something back.

Emma sat on the thick carpet in Eve's small office, solemnly reading a brightly coloured picture-book, ignoring their discussion. Three years was the length of her life to date: she was being offered her entire lifetime, repeated. Her parents sat watching her, breathing a little more easily. For the moment they could fall no further; they could even permit themselves a small ration of hope. A cure might well be found in three years. A marrow donor might even be found, although Eve was as frank as always on this: odd blood-lines in Rick's family — a Finnish great-grandparent — had left the child with a rare tissue-type, possibly unique.

'Of course we'll type you both,' she said. 'And Ben. And all the grandparents, if they're willing.'

'Of *course* they're willing.'

'You'd be surprised — sometimes family members refuse.'

They were surprised to hear this, very surprised, but the issue was unimportant, and irrelevant to their overriding concern.

'I don't want to raise false hopes,' Eve said. 'I have to warn you that a match is very unlikely.'

Driving home afterwards Linda cried the tears she had been suppressing for days, but softly, to herself and to Rick, maintaining conversation as best she could, trying not to disturb the little girl strapped into the back seat.

'Whassa matter, Mummy?'

'I'm a bit sad, Wol.'

'Why, Mummy?'

'Mummy's sad because you're not more ugly,' Rick said, through his own choked throat, and the sudden thought, strange and magical, reappearing after many years, surprised Linda into the glimmer of a smile, despite her pain.

Emma stared out the window, completely satisfied, as if her question had not required an answer that made sense, merely an utterance.

'I want an icecream, Daddy?'

'So do I, Wol.'

4.

In the months that followed there was much for those wide Wol eyes to take in. The little girl's life now revolved about the hospital. Giant scanners periodically engulfed and disgorged her; sharp needles pricked her tiny thumb-pads daily; various drug-combinations made her ill, or made her hair fall out – made her, Rick joked, once, bitterly, 'almost ugly'.

Mostly, hospital life was a life of waiting, in bright primary-coloured ante-rooms filled with picture books and soft toys. Her parents often wondered what she made of it all – what exactly was going on behind those solemn owl-eyes. At the age of three, her understanding of death was limited. A pet goldfish had once been buried in the backyard with due ceremony under a small twig cross, then promptly forgotten. On another occasion, tears filling her eyes, she had chased away a neighbour's cat that was tormenting a spring fledgeling on the back lawn. As if choosing to torment *her* instead, the cat had returned under cover of darkness and left a pair of tiny, stiff, inedible wings amid a scatter of soft down on the grass: a deliberate and malevolent gift, it seemed, for the little girl to find in the morning. Various species of squashed wildlife that lined the road to a beach-holiday one summer had caused less misery – 'road pizza' Benjamin had called it, repeatedly, trying to shock his sister, but only making her giggle.

At four, during her first remission, there was a flurry of bedtime questions. *How old will you be when you die, Mummy? Will you go to heaven?*

The little girl had never appeared concerned by her illness while actually ill, but perhaps – her hair was growing back, and she was gaining weight – she now half-sensed that she was past it, and it was safe to ask such questions. The subject of death would disappear within weeks, Eve Harrison reassured the worried parents.

'It's just a phase. A normal, healthy phase.'

'But what do we *tell* her?'

'Tell her the truth. Tell her what you would like to hear in her place. These are normal four-year-old questions.'

Less normal was an awareness of her own mortality that emerged, obliquely, when signs of the disease returned the following year: a self-awareness that was bent, at first, into an obsession with the health of her grandparents, with the signs of age and deterioration of their bodies.

She burst into tears in the car, without warning, driving home, after a Sunday visit to Rick's parents.

'I don't want Grandma to die,' she blubbered.

Rick turned to face her, alarmed: 'She's not going to die, Wol — not for a long time. She's only fifty years old.'

'But her *hair* is so old. '

The child's own bald head — the scorched-earth of chemotherapy — was concealed by a bright, batik scarf. Linda, who was driving, stopped the car; Rick climbed out and into the backseat with Emma, Ben squeezed over the gear-shift into the front.

They drove on with the father nursing his daughter.

'No-one is going to die, Wol,' he murmured. 'Not Grandma. Not anyone. Not for a long time. In our family everyone lives to be a hundred years old. *Every* one.'

But these were her own anxieties, self-anxieties, once-removed; they could not be reasoned away.

'Are you going to be cremated or buried, Grandma?' she blurted across the dinner table the following Sunday.

Forewarned, the grandmother — a youthful fifty-five — laughed, lightly: 'It's so far away I haven't thought about it, Wol.'

The small girl watched her solemnly for a time.

'If you're cremated,' she finally said. 'You might not have a body to wear in heaven.'

The adults smiled at each other above her head, allowing themselves to be amused, *willing* themselves to be amused — but breathing a little more easily when Emma pushed herself away from the table and slipped off to play.

The deeper question — the blunt question they had all dreaded — took several more months to find its way through this maze of detours and displacements.

'Am I going to die, Mummy?'

Linda had woken around dawn to find Emma standing at the bedside, gazing down at her. Early birds twittered outside, the first light of morning was sneaking between the curtain-chinks. She pulled aside the quilt, the little girl clambered up and in. Rick, waking more slowly, rolled to face them; the daughter lay nestled between her parents, her big owl-eyes glistening in the half-dark, gathering what little light there was. Her voice when she spoke was matter-of-fact, unafraid – having finally reached this destination she was far less concerned, it seemed, for herself, than she had been, months earlier, for the health of her grandmothers.

'Will I go to heaven?'

'Of course. One day. Not for a long time.'

More questions followed: 'What will I do there? What will I do on my own? Who will look after me?'

She had clearly been preparing a list for some time.

'You won't be on your own, Wol. I'll already be there. Grandma will already be there. We'll all be together.'

'What if I can't find you? What if I'm not allowed to see you?'

'Why wouldn't you find us?'

'Because I've been naughty.'

A catalogue of tiny misdemeanours followed; she was easily reassured that none was unforgivable. Having emptied herself, methodically, of these preoccupations she fell almost instantly asleep, leaving her parents facing each other, staring at each other in the half-dark of the morning, their warm breaths mingling, their thoughts desperately agitating.

5.

'Worry achieves nothing,' Eve attempted to reassure the young parents. 'Worry is useless, a total waste of energy.'

There was nothing wasteful about Eve Harrison: her hair cropped short, her face free of make-up. Her clothes — plain smock, sensible flat-heeled shoes — also seemed blunt, functional, to the point. Unadorned.

But the two parents increasingly wanted adornment, they wanted to hear reassuring fibs, or at least half-truths. Their need for bluntness had passed; they now wanted cosmetics. Despite Eve's advice to the contrary, they had also come to depend on worry. Worrying was far from useless, they sensed: the worry process was a restless working through of possibilities and permutations, an exhaustive examination of every path, every fork in the path. Rick, grown accustomed to insomnia over the years of Emma's illness, had come to think of those long hours of tossing and turning and worrying in bed as a search programme: a brute-search, like a computer chess-game he had bought, as a birthday present to himself, some years before. The game had obsessed him. He had glued himself to the video display, fascinated, every night for weeks, as the programme checked the consequences of every possible move, counted possibilities, eliminated dead-ends in the maze of infinite possible end-games.

Worry was also a kind of fuel, he suspected: a higher-octane fuel, for a higher temperature furnace. It raised the metabolic rate, it provided the energy that kept them both going, that was channelled into doing things, into actual physical tasks: the keeping of temperature charts, the counting of bruises, the frequent phone-calls to Eve, the trips to the hospital. It got them through the day – through the routines of each day. It also got them through the weeks, and months, and years, powering more optimistic, longer-range tasks: the correspondence that Rick began with tissue-banks and bone-marrow registers around the world, Linda's volunteer work with the Make-a-Wish Foundation, and the Leukaemia Support Group.

At first resistant to these groups – unwilling to admit that Emma might ever come to need last wishes, or support — she was dragged along to an Annual General Meeting by another parent, a mother she had met in the same bright waiting-rooms, and found herself nominated onto the support group's fund-raising committee. Soon she was immersed completely, finding relief, and even satisfaction, in taking down the minutes, typing the monthly newsletter, xeroxing and mailing copies. She was, she felt, at last helping her child, expending all that accumulated worry-energy usefully: a small cog in the wheel of Cure.

When the search for paths into the future ended in a blind-alley, there was still the past to examine. The feeling was inescapable that they were somehow to blame, that it might even help if they were to blame. Had Linda taken some harmful drug during pregnancy? Drunk one glass too many of wine? Had there been something else in Emma's childhood environment — something chemical, or unnatural, against which they had failed to protect her? If they could not blame themselves, they blamed others. Linda's father — a heavy smoker, two packs a day — came under suspicion briefly.

'It's such a filthy habit, Dad,' Linda berated him one Sunday, over a family meal. 'If you won't think of yourself, think of others. I'm not saying it has anything to do with Wol — but who knows?'

Rick, unwilling to criticise his father-in-law directly, and specifically, told a more general story in the silence which followed.

'I was at a curriculum meeting a few weeks ago. In at Head Office. There was only one smoker in the room. Jenny Adams — the chairperson — asked him to put out his cigarette. When he refused, she stood up, leaned across the table and — I kid you not — spat on him.'

His father-in-law was incredulous: 'She *what?*'

'She spat on him.'

'That's disgusting.'

'Maybe. I don't say I agree with it. But I think we'll see more of it. If he pollutes her, she said, then she was going to pollute him.'

Linda's mother, quiet till that point — quiet, it could be said, for many years till that point, a gentle and generous woman — but now seething with anger, finally spoke up.

'I feel that *you* have spat on your father,' she said to Linda, and through Linda also to Rick. 'Here tonight. You have spat on him in his own house. I don't like smoking any more than you, but to suggest it might have something to do with Wol — well, I think it's the most horrible thing you have ever said.'

Apologies followed, by phone, over several days; normal relations were gradually resumed.

Despite Eve's frequent reassurances, and advice, such obsessions consumed the next few years, and consumed them at speed. If three years was to be their remaining time with their daughter, it was passing too quickly.

'Remember those interminable Beowulf lectures,' Rick murmured in bed one night. 'I used to think if I had a week left to live, I'd spend the entire week in Beowulf lectures. It would make the time last forever.'

'You think we should take it up again?'

'Time is passing too quickly. I look up and another month has vanished.'

'But that's another month she's survived.'

Their older, gentler routines — nightly book-readings, weekend picnics — were becoming episodic, haphazard, disrupted by their new obsessions and schedules. Even Church attendance was disrupted. At first, the boyish John Cummings and his ancient congregation had been discreetly supportive as word of Emma's illness spread. Now, when the family did get to church, it was such an event, and such a fuss was made of Emma — so much consolation and pity and even, once, public prayers, were offered — that it became an ordeal.

'Never again,' Linda vowed, as they drove away one Sunday.

Rick defended the young priest: 'He didn't mention her by name.'

'But he was looking directly *at* her. How could he do that? Without even asking us?'

The children sat in the back seat, listening. They had heard the prayers, absorbed the sympathetic smiles of the congregation – there seemed little point in excluding them from the discussion.

'Aren't we going to church anymore?' Ben asked.

'Not for a while.'

'But I want to go. Emma doesn't have to come if she doesn't want to – but I want to go.'

'We don't have time, Ben,' his father said, firmly.

Always more difficult than his placid sister, the boy now demanded even more of their attention, as if to keep his share constant, or proportionate. At times he seemed almost jealous of his sister's disease. Over the years he had been the sickly one, the designated patient, now he was forced to compete for a place on the sickbed. Most mornings he complained of aches in the belly or chest or head. He frequently missed school, he insisted on accompanying the family to hospital, he demanded that Doctor Eve examine *his* ears or throat, press her cold stethoscope against his chest.

On one memorable visit he even demanded that he, too, be given a needle.

Eve – grown tired of his pestering – was more than happy to oblige. She filled a syringe with saline solution, and attached the largest-bore needle she could find. At the sight of that horse-needle, aimed in his direction, the boy changed his mind and fled from the room, amid laughter.

6.

At six, approaching the three-year survival milestone, the odds seemed to have altered in Emma's favour.

'To have come this far,' Rick asked Eve, or perhaps begged her, during their weekly visit, 'surely that gives her an even greater chance?'

Eve still had no time for false hope: 'It *might* mean she has even less. She has used up her allotted span.'

Her bluntness, which had once seemed an asset – if only because they knew she would never lie to them – on this occasion seemed merely cruel. Rick shivered, a sudden involuntary spasm; Linda reached out and touched the polished wood of Eve's desk. It was not the first time she had resorted to such gestures; gazing down on her sleeping daughter only a few nights before, she had found herself trying not to think how beautiful the child was, and had begun reciting maths tables aloud, trying to jam her mind against the thought. She studied the Sagittarian predictions of the horoscope column each morning, feeling a flood of stupid gratitude whenever good health or long life was promised. She imposed a series of diets, many suggested by her mother, on the entire family for months at a time – Pritikin, Vegan, gluten-free, yeast-free, Feingold – each time reverting to the meaty, yeasty, fatty norm when Emma herself finally complained.

Neither the protective magic of astrologers and diets, nor the prayers offered up in Church, could ward off the greater power of statistics, and the laws of probability. The disease returned a few months later; 'active treatment' was stopped shortly afterwards, after a last failure of response to chemotherapy. The phrase, and its coy replacement – 'palliative treatment' – seemed out-of-character for Eve Harrison: an evasion, which in itself told the parents of the seriousness of Emma's plight.

'The effects of further treatment would be worse than the disease,' she added, when pressed.

'There must be *something*.'

'We can offer transfusions if her blood count falls too low. We can control bleeding, and infections . . . But no more chemotherapy.'

Eve glanced down at her desk, at a sheaf of blood-screens that she had surely checked several times before: another uncharacteristic avoidance.

'The time she has left isn't long,' she said. 'I see no point in making her suffer unnecessarily.'

The parents held each other's gaze, waiting for the other to act as spokesperson, waiting for one of their mouths to speak the thought.

'*How* long?' Linda eventually asked

'A few weeks. Four. Six. It's difficult to be precise.'

Linda reached out her hand, Rick clasped it tightly.

'I promise that she will be comfortable,' Eve said. 'I promise that she will feel no pain. But that's all I can promise.'

7.

There was no time for hysterics, or further recriminations. Even tears seemed a luxury, an indulgence that had to be postponed.

Until.

One question had to be answered rationally, and immediately: how to spend those last few weeks together, how to make them at least halfway happy. The idea of a Last Wish trip to Disneyland or Disney World in America – or even to the cluster of smaller, closer Lands and Worlds on the Queensland Gold Coast – was repellent to both parents: bread and circuses.

What did you do afterwards, they asked each other? What did you do after closing time on the last day in Disneyland, pushing out through the exit-turnstiles in a queue of weary parents and overtired children? Surely that was a kind of death itself, and to pin happiness on such a last wish was to die two deaths.

'Imagine the flight back home. Like riding a tumbril to the guillotine. Much better to do nothing special. To spend these last weeks in our ordinary, everyday way.'

By the time they had argued this through – and changed their minds, and agreed to override their squeamishness if it was Emma's wish – her weakness and fragility did not permit such long distance trips.

Or so Eve Harrison told them. Eve was still their sole confidante; for the moment they decided to keep all four grandparents in the dark, or half-dark; avoiding constant visits, constant fussing. Above all, they sought normalcy, they sought to restore the family games, the music, the book-readings of an earlier, happier, more mundane life. Perhaps they also half-believed that a return to these routines might magically transport them back through time, or at least allow them to pretend that they were still back there, that the intervening horror had never occurred.

'You know what I miss most?' Rick whispered in his wife's ear one night.

They lay in bed together, spoon-nestled, having made love for the first time in many weeks, although more as an antidote for insomnia than out of love, or lust. The cure, like all others, had failed.

'What do you miss?'

'The opportunity to be bored. Like when we were first married.'

She almost laughed. 'I used to *bore* you?'

'Bad choice of words. You know what I mean. Having an empty mind every now and then. Not having this . . . *thing* always there, inside.'

'I miss how we used to read to each other. When Ben was a baby. How just the sound of the words would soothe him.'

'*Sedate* him, you mean.'

She shrugged in his arms. 'Perhaps we need such sedation ourselves.'

She lay there for a moment longer, then rose, and felt her way to the door, and turned on the light. He watched her, naked in the sudden glare, standing at the bedroom bookshelves – every room in their house was filled with bookshelves – head-tilted, reading the spines.

'Where shall we start?'

'You had finished Middlemarch,' he said. 'You were working your way through Dickens – again.'

'It's so long ago I can't remember.'

'I remember,' he said, and they both managed a small laugh.

'You're still not a fan?'

'I didn't like his last one,' he said, and they laughed again.

'We never read *A Tale of Two Cities*,' she told him.

'I saw the film when I was a boy. A long time ago. I must have been eight or nine – but I remember it clearly.'

Head still tilted, she searched the close-packed shelves as he talked.

'My father took me,' he was saying. 'I was amazed – he never went to the movies. Sorry – the *pictures*. He always said they numbed the mind.'

'A man after my own heart.'

'Even more amazing – it was on a week night. We never went *any*where on week nights. And suddenly he arrived home from work and announced he was taking me to the pictures. Just me. It was an old film – black and white. I can't remember who was in it.'

'Charles Darnay and Sydney Carton.'

'The actors in the film?'

Linda laughed; she had been teasing him: 'The characters in the book.'

He wasn't listening to her; he was back in time, reliving that glowing night: 'I still remember the last scene. The hero climbs the steps, the guillotine waits. He makes a very moving speech – or maybe he only thinks the words. And suddenly he's lifted above it all – the guillotine, the basket of heads, the bloodthirsty mob, it's all a long way away, far *below* him. I had goose-bumps all over. I must have been about Ben's age.'

'I wouldn't take Ben to it,' she said. 'Nine is too young. It would give him nightmares.'

'It's not really violent,' he said. 'Not by today's standards. And it meant a lot to me – I'd forgotten how much. Maybe I'll take him to the movies again when he's older.'

He paused: they both realised that they were talking about a child with a future. They were already talking about him as if he were an only child. They had broken an unspoken rule: that it was unfair to their daughter to make plans that did not include her, that were beyond her.

'I know what the book looks like,' Linda said, as she continued to search the shelves. 'It's not part of the set. Olive-green binding – very old, a little tatty.'

'Maybe it's in the lounge.'

But she tugged the book from some deep recess, blew dust from the pages, then turned immediately to the last page, and began to read: '*It is a far, far better thing I do than I have ever done; it is a far, far better rest I go to than I have ever had.*'

They sat, silenced, sharing the same thought: that each would willingly, gladly, take the place of their small daughter in the tumbril. And yet they were powerless. They would have donated a kidney or lung to save her – they would have donated both lungs, they would each have sacrificed a still-beating *heart* – but their bone marrow, the only gift she needed, spread plentifully through their bodies, in far, far greater quantities than they would ever require themselves, was useless, even fatally dangerous to her.

8.

In the following weeks Emma slowly became aware, again, of the existence of that tumbril in which she was riding, of the fact that it had turned a last corner, and the square ahead, and all it contained, had come into view. Had some developmental threshold been crossed in her growth? A spurt in the imagination, or brain-size, which permitted her to clearly see the future, or the absence of future, for the first time? Or had she had come to sense, and be infected by, the desperation of her parents, which they always tried to shield from her? The attentions of her grandparents, fully briefed, finally, on the extent of her predicament, were a further cue. Her stoic, wise-owl manner vanished for longer intervals, and resisted jolting back to equilibrium. When she sat with her books, or paints, or drawing-pads, her gaze was often fixed to one side, defocussed.

Morbid fascination fuelled her talk at meal-times: endless questions about bones, dust, ashes, cremation, coffins. She solemnly examined the blue-black bruises that appeared on her body, at times even measured those bruises with her school ruler in a parody of one of the earlier obsessions of her parents.

As the end also became clearer to Rick and Linda, they resumed church-going, choosing to look pity in the eye, to stare it down. In part this return to the fold was still a search for the routines of normality, an attempt to travel backwards in time; in part it was a last desperate reaching out — not for miracles, perhaps, but at least for answers. Each Sunday at St Paul's they huddled together in a back pew, in a far corner, wanting only a private, family worship, a communion between them and whatever God might haunt the old stone church. Privacy was not so easy: once again the Reverend Cummings insisted on intervening and mediating — translating — between them and that God. He asked for shared prayers from the congregation, mentioned their trials in sermons; and after Rick protested — politely, but firmly — began visiting them at home instead, uninvited.

'Don't forget the power of faith,' he exhorted over innumerable cups of tea. 'The power of prayer.'

Linda had reached exasperation point.

'I don't understand,' she said, 'why that would help. And if it did — what kind of God would insist on it? Why should we have to *beg* for favours?'

He sat back in an armchair — Rick's leather armchair, appropriated — and pursed his lips and pressed his fingertips together. More at home in the pulpit lecturing his flock on issues of social justice – poverty, land rights, unemployment – he seemed lost in the world of personal, immediate pain. He might have been enacting a role, playing a part meant for someone older: a wise uncle, or grandfather.

'I don't want to sound glib,' he murmured, 'But if we knew all the answers – if knowledge was given to us on a plate – what would be the point of faith?'

'That's fine advice for us,' she said. 'But what do we tell *her*? Jesus wants her for a sunbeam?'

'Perhaps she doesn't want to be told anything,' he said. 'In many ways this is far more difficult test for you.'

'What you are saying – this is a test? This was given to us as a test of *faith*? What's the answer? Is it an essay, or multi-choice?'

He paused before answering, shocked by her harshness. He licked his lips, his mouth opened and closed, without speaking, groping for an answer that was not quite ready. He was out of his depth, or had forgotten his lines. His avuncular manner had vanished, his eyes reddened, he was close to tears. He mumbled a few words about eternal peace, about Emma going to a better world, but they could plainly hear that his heart wasn't in it; he was of their generation, skeptical of the unknown. His heaven was on earth, and would be manmade, if at all.

'Remember the story of Abraham and Isaac?' he finally said, huskily. 'The Lord tested Abraham's faith by asking him to sacrifice his son?'

Despite his anguish, Linda's face purpled with rage, instantly.

'Fuck you,' she said. 'And fuck any God who would play such horrible games.'

Rick rose from his chair, unastonished by the words she had spoken, even though he had never heard her utter such words before, or even seen such an extreme of anger. The same feelings, if not the same words, were on the tip of his own tongue; there was nothing else that could be felt.

'Perhaps I didn't choose my example well. What I meant to say . . .'

'I think we've talked enough, John,' Rick said. 'We'd like to be alone.'

As they stood at the door, holding each other, watching Father Cummings drive away for the last time, they realised suddenly how much they had aged in the past months, at a much faster rate than their household clocks and calendars had measured out.

It seemed that this young priest, approximately their own age, now belonged to a still younger generation.

'It's up to us,' Rick said to his wife. 'No-one can help except us.'

9.

The priest's words of advice stuck fast in their minds, nevertheless, like a tune heard once in the morning that can't be shaken off, repeating, interminably, through the day. The possibility that it was somehow an ordeal, a trial, was difficult to shake loose, if only because of its deeper implication: it pandered to the hope of a solution. Their powerlessness was deformed into guilt, which was bent itself into over-attentiveness, into a smothery kind of love that the little girl was forced sometimes to turn away from, to physically *hide* from. Famine-thin, increasingly fragile, easily bruised, it was as if she sensed that her parents might cuddle her to death, or at least cuddle her back into hospital. She shut herself in her room for long periods, alone, and — it seemed to Rick and Linda, in their worst moments — betrayed.

'It's as if there's a wall there — we're on one side, she's on the other.'

'We can't help her — but I think she thinks we *won't* help her.'

The worry-programme had bypassed one possible solution, or pathway, much earlier, but goaded by guilt, and self-blame, returned to it, was dragged back to it, again and again — although for some time neither discussed the path with the other, believing that for the first time in their marriage their thoughts had diverged too widely, that the idea was so outrageous, so *unspeakable*, that no two sane people would ever think it together.

Rick first spoke the unspeakable. They lay talking in bed in the small hours, trying, as always, to talk each other to sleep, to talk themselves empty, to talk out the day's accumulated worries. A volume of Dickens lay discarded on the floor; another waif had died; he had become unreadable.

'Maybe we should all go together,' he said, inserting the words suddenly, without warning, into a lull in a conversation about household finances.

'What do you mean?'

'Just that. We shouldn't let her go . . . alone.'

'You mean . . . we should go *with* her?'

Linda's tone was surprisingly calm; he peered at her through the half-dark, trying to read her face.

'You don't seem surprised,' he murmured.

'It crossed my mind too. I've thought of it several times. I've tried *not* to think it — it seemed too crazy.'

She shivered in his arms: a convulsion that was more a shudder of disgust. He shivered himself, contagiously.

'It *is* crazy,' he said. 'It's crazy even to talk about it.'

She rolled away from him, but he followed, pressing against her from behind: 'There's Ben to think of, if nothing else,' she murmured. 'What right would we have to take him with us?'

Even now, the idea was only half speakable, couched in the euphemisms of travel and journeys. Of family holidays.

'He would hate to be left out,' Rick said, and they both suddenly laughed, briefly, too-loudly, then lay together for some minutes in silence, their bodies stilled, their hearts pounding, not quite believing that such thoughts had crept out into the open.

The subject of Ben had opened another door, the worry-programme had thrown up another weird solution, only slightly less unspeakable. This time it was Linda who found the words:

'Maybe only one of us should go with her. Maybe I should go with her.'

Rick rolled apart from her: 'You want me to lose *both* of you?

'Is your grief going to be worse?' she said. 'Could it *be* any worse?'

'Of course it would be worse.'

She could hear the doubt in his voice; she knew that he was already there, ahead, or at least abreast of her.

More long, slow minutes, then she spoke, as of old, for them both: 'Are two griefs worse than one? How much worse can it be? Can things be worse than *worst*?'

Their hearts pounded on as they lay there at rest, in bed. Sweat broke out across Rick's face, his hands shook, the sheets were damp and clammy against his skin. The darkness, crowding and claustrophobic, surrounded him; it seemed a viscous element, heavy on his senses, preventing clear thought.

'This is absurd,' he said. 'We'll have other children. We can have another baby straight away.'

'It's not us we're talking about,' Linda said.

He lay in silence, rebuked.

'It's Wol,' she continued. 'I can't bear to think of her going away – alone. It's as though we've cast her out into the woods. Abandoned her, like something in a fairy-tale. And we won't go with her.'

She paused; the idea was growing, taking more definite shape: 'I *want* to go with her,' she announced, more definitely.

'I don't want to hear any more about it,' Rick said.

'It's late — we're both exhausted. In the clear light of day you'll realise how crazy this is.'

'Just think about it,' she urged. 'That's all I ask.'

He rolled away from her, to the far side of the bed, out of contact.

'No,' he said, angrily. 'I won't. Not ever. I don't want to hear about it again.'

10.

As the child's immune system failed, she was fed an exotic daily salad of antibiotics to prevent infection; these in turn suppressed her appetite, she lost weight steadily. She rapidly came to resemble the snapshots of her forgotten foster siblings in Bangladesh and Ecuador: all skin and bones, her eyes sunk deeply into their dark sockets. Her period of self-isolation had passed, she now preferred to sleep in her parents' bed each night, between them, facing her father — which meant that they slept even less themselves, anxious not to squash her frail bird-bones, or bruise her paper-thin skin. Often Linda would leave father and daughter together, sneaking off into Emma's room, or into Ben's room, spending the night squeezed even more uncomfortably into the narrow bed of a boy who was as unwilling as ever to be left out.

And as Rick lay there, sleepless, his daughter's small milky breath puffing rhythmically into his face, the realisation grew: that if their lunatic plan was ever followed through, if someone did choose to go with her, of course it would be him, not Linda.

Night-thoughts, certainly, bred of insomnia and despair — but he was beginning to suspect that despair was the default state of the human mind, if normally hidden from the mind by lack of imagination, or the balms of warmth and food and love.

This, at least, was clear: the child would want *him* with her at the end, it was his presence that would most reassure her.

He decided, for the moment, to keep this realisation to himself.

Eve Harrison was visiting the house daily at the time, checking Emma's temperature, listening to her chest, peering into orifices. And still pricking her thumb-pads every second or third visit, siphoning tiny drops of blood

'Does she have to go through this?' Linda asked, although the needles seemed to bother her more than her stoical daughter.

Several times Eve urged hospitalisation, but both parents had decided that Emma would die — although they still couldn't bring themselves to utter the blunt word – at home, in a familiar world, believing it would be her own wish.

Home had one other advantage, unspoken: although no decision had yet been made, and their lunatic plan had not been discussed again, both knew that it would be impossible to carry out in hospital.

'How can hospital help her?' Linda demanded of her friend.

'She may need a transfusion. Depending on the blood count.'

'Couldn't she be transfused at home?'

Eve was reluctant to agree, but it was the reluctance of fixed habits: 'I suppose I could arrange a home-care nurse,' she conceded.

This was not enough for Linda: 'I can do whatever needs to be done – I'm sure I can. With your help, of course.'

'It's a 24-hour job. When will you sleep? She will need constant nursing attention.'

'We'll work in shifts. I'll sleep when Rick is awake.'

'A night-nurse, then. Someone to keep watch overnight. Please, you can't do it all yourself.'

Rick, listening to the debate, intervened: 'We don't want to share the remaining time with strangers, Eve. Surely you can understand that?'

Eve, ever practical, quickly realised that to argue with these stubborn parents was a waste of time. A crash course in basic nursing procedures followed, under her supervision. True to her promise, she left a stash of pain-killing liquids and suppositories, and several syringes and ampoules of stronger stuff, with written instructions on dosage schedules. An impromptu lecture on the properties and uses of each drug was followed by a kind of brief oral exam, or viva – delivered with Eve's characteristic efficiency. This in turn was followed by a practical tutorial: she arrived one morning with a bag of big navel oranges, and had her two mature-age students slipping small butterfly needles through the skin of the fruit, getting the 'feel'.

'There should be no need for these,' Eve said. 'But just in case. If she bleeds, I can instruct you by phone on what to give.'

Having passed the orange-test, they moved onto human flesh: jabbing needles into each other's veins, repeatedly, under Eve's scrutiny. There was an odd relief in this, a mix of slapstick comedy and pain, that provided, temporarily, a release from their preoccupations.

'Stick to the dose I've suggested,' Eve advised, leaving. 'These are powerful drugs. Too much could be fatal.'

Rick wondered for a moment if she were suggesting the exact opposite, subtly: offering them a final pain-relief for Emma — a final safety net. Although of course Eve had no inkling of the full extent of their hidden agenda.

An agenda that was still half-hidden, also, from each other. Their minds were moving in parallel: along true parallel lines, never touching. Rick, especially, refused to admit that he was still giving the matter thought. At times the plan seemed outrageously stupid — even the simple sums were so wrong. At other times it seemed inevitable, logical — even if it was the logic of despair.

Finally, discussion could be deferred no more: an oblique mention by Linda began a series of escalating arguments. Soon they were debating, whispering heatedly, each night in bed — and thinking up counter-arguments in silence all day, with Ben at school, but with Emma, too fragile now for school, always hovering at brink of ear-shot. At first these discussions were in subjunctive mode, preceded by an 'if' or a 'should'; this kept the unspeakable hypothetical, and permitted a discussion of the plan — The Plan — as if it were science-fiction, or a kind of algebra which dealt with symbols rather than with real people and real events, yet still allowed a plan of action to be fleshed out, and modified, and tested.

'*If* we told her,' Linda said, 'that you were going with her, then we could never change our minds. We could never take it back. We would have to be absolutely certain before we could tell her.'

Behind these abstractions there was a mounting urgency, for time was short. Emma, too, appeared to sense this. She began sleeping poorly; refusing to go to bed, to any bed, even to her parents' bed. She actively resisted sleep. Rick and Linda would wake at night to hear her padding about the house, or softly singing songs in the dark bed between them. Once they were woken by the dazzle of the bedlamp to find her propped up between them in bed, reading.

'I don't feel tired,' she explained.

When pressed to turn out the light and shut her eyes, she burst into tears: 'What if I don't wake up?'

'One day, Wol,' Rick told her, 'you will wake up and you will be in heaven. You will close your eyes, here on earth, and when you open them you will be somewhere else.'

They lay together in bed, the small girl cuddled between her parents. The emotion of the moment stripped bare the cliches he was speaking, freed them from trite associations. They were, simply, the only words that could be uttered.

Rick's heart pounded, he prepared himself to speak again, to force out the next words, knowing that once they were uttered they were a promise, binding and irrevocable. As he opened his mouth, Linda suddenly reached over and gripped his arm.

'Don't,' she said, 'Please. We need more time to think it through.'

11.

From that night every light in the house was left burning – especially Ben's bedroom light. But Emma's fear of the dark, also, flushed her parents' discussions out into the open, into the light, from behind the cover of hypothetical ifs and shoulds.

'We need counselling,' Linda stated. 'That we could even *contemplate* it – don't you think we're a bit mad? That we need some sort of help?'

'No,' he said. 'I mean – yes, maybe we are mad. But no – no counselling. They'd take her away from us. They'd take them *both* from us.'

'But we've lost perspective. We're irrational – so caught up in this we can't see the wood for the trees.'

'Maybe that's the best perspective.'

To some extent the two sides of these debates were interchangeable: pro and con arguments were rotated between them. The deeper disagreement was not between the two parents, but within each of them.

'It's such a weight,' Linda said. 'If we could at least *talk* it over with someone. With friends.'

'Which friends? Who could we possibly burden with this? I wouldn't wish it on my worst enemy.'

In this fashion, passed back and forth, like a shared load, too hot or too heavy to handle alone, it was slowly decided. When their daughter next burst into tears, and refused to risk sleep, and Rick opened his mouth, Linda held her peace, allowing him to speak.

The words still took some time to emerge, they seemed stuck to the dry roof of his mouth.

'When you die, Wol,' he said. 'Whenever it is, I will be there with you. I am going to die before you.'

Her tears had vanished; she watched him, curious.

'How do you know that?'

'I can make myself die,' he told her. 'With an injection. I'm going to die first, so I'll be there waiting for you.'

And so there could be no turning back, no chickening out, no abandoning her if she went first.

This also had been planned – that she was to see him dead, to *know* him dead, before she died herself.

A calm gravity returned to her face. She asked a few further questions – technical questions – then within minutes her wide Wol-eyes closed, and she was sleeping, snuggled against her father's still-pounding heart. He realised that she took it for granted that he would choose to die with her; it was a wonderful comfort to her, yes, but his intended sacrifice – a sacrifice of everything – meant nothing else to her. He saw no selfishness in her reaction, not even the normal self-centredness of a child, but an entirely reasonable interpretation of events to an intelligent six-year-old mind: if heaven was such a wonderful place, why wouldn't he choose to come too?

His own view of the road ahead was a little more terrifying. And yet – at the same time, once the decision had been made, and was locked in place – oddly exciting. A far, far better place? He doubted it. Whatever faith he had once had now seemed shallow: a routine, social faith. He felt he was going nowhere, just ending – but perhaps those last few days, and especially nights, of peace, would make it worthwhile. And perhaps, just *perhaps* . . .

'You know the cemetery's a bit like home to me,' he whispered to his wife, in bed.

She set aside the book she was reading, and looked at him, disturbed, uncertain of his tone: 'Rick – don't be morbid.'

'No – I've been there before. As a boy. I once spent a Saturday night in the local graveyard – camping with a friend.'

She listened, reluctantly. Once such a story would have surprised her, now it seemed little more than tame; she knew that both of them had depths that were darker and weirder than had once seemed possible.

'It was his idea,' Rick was saying. 'We each told our parents we were staying at the other's. We took our sleeping bags, and lay there most of the night, among the gravestones, telling ghost stories, trying to terrify ourselves.'

She shivered: 'You must have been crazy.'

'It was a dare – you had to do it. But it was an anticlimax. Suddenly it was morning – we must have slept – and nothing had happened. Of course we were heroes at school – we made up all kinds of horror stories. But deep down I was disappointed. It was the end of something – the end of the tooth-fairy. There just wasn't anything out there – no other dimension. There were no ghosts.'

12.

Ben was told of the plan — after further intense discussion — the following night. Both parents were unsure what he would make of it, had even worried that he might demand to go too, jealous to the end of the way his entire world had come to orbit another, different focal point: his younger sister.

To him, their explanation was subjunctive again, peppered with ifs and maybes and even with the outright lie that the decision was not yet made, and what did he, Ben, think?

The boy moved to his mother's side, and held tightly to her, and watched his father for some time, for once silent and undemanding, unable to fully grasp what was being said to him, but sensing its gravity. Rick prattled on, talking far too quickly, telling his son that one day they would be together again, all of them, that until then he would have to look after his mother, that he would be the man of the house.

The boy stared at him, uncomprehending — perhaps, even at nine, disbelieving. Explanations that had sounded profound the night before — talk of journeys, of waking in heaven, of future meetings — now sounded banal, or untrue, or even meaningless.

Not for the first time, panic overwhelmed Rick, a wave of terror at the enormity, and absurdity, of the scheme. For the first time also — as his son watched him, suspiciously — he wondered also at the long-term effects it would surely have on the boy. Agitated, emptied of words, he left him with Linda, and swallowed a sleeping pill that Eve had prescribed for both of them some months before — knowing that he wouldn't sleep, but that at least he might be calmed. Later, in the silence of the very smallest hours, as the rest of the household slept, he rose from his bed, and spent much of the night writing a series of letters to his son: letters to be opened yearly, posthumously, on each successive birthday. He began with simple declarations of love — messages to a little boy from his father in heaven — then for the later years a gradually more complex mix of explanations and exhortations, and, finally, requests for forgiveness. He tried to recall his own states of mind, his own level of development, at various ages — ten, thirteen, sixteen — and tailor his messages accordingly. This was not as difficult as it first seemed: the chronology of the letters, splashed here and there with tears, followed, simply, the evolving complexity of his own thoughts as the long night progressed. The earlier letters to a younger Ben were drafts for the more subtle and sophisticated versions that the boy would open as he grew older.

You are 18, it's been a year since we last talked, and this is the last time we will talk. I hope these letters have not been a burden to you — hauntings from an old ghost. You are nearly as old as I was when you were born, writing this, and it would seem presumptuous to offer any more guidance . . .

Sometime before dawn he heard Linda rise and begin moving about in the kitchen. He finished the last letter, and joined her outside on the back terrace. She was sitting at the garden table with a pot of coffee and two cups, clearly expecting him.

He seemed to have spent all his agitation of the night before; extruded it, poured it into that pile of letters. The outside world was starkly defined: sharp silhouettes and edges, a world of knife-edge clarity. An early bird glided between trees in a neighbour's backyard; the cool air was so still that Rick imagined he could feel the trace of its passage: a faint stirring of wings, a spreading ripple.

Perhaps the tranquillity of the morning seduced them, lulled them into the belief that their plan was not as difficult or as stupid as it had often seemed. Sitting there, holding hands, sipping coffee as light slowly flooded the eastern sky, they decided, almost matter-of-factly, as if scribbling a dental appointment in a diary, on the date.

13.

On the second-to-last evening the four grandparents were invited to dinner. They arrived bearing gifts: big soft toys, chocolates for the children. There were no gifts for Rick; he watched, wistfully, as his parents and parents-in-law spent the evening fussing over Ben and Emma, careful to share their attentions, and their gifts, equally. There was no way of telling them what was planned, or receiving his due share of that attention. There was no proper way of saying goodbye.

Linda brought her father an ashtray as they sat in the family room, sipping pre-dinner drinks, but he declared that he had given up.

'Weeks ago,' his wife added, mildly. 'It's the one good thing to come out of all this.'

The evening ended with offers from both grandmothers to stay in the house 'until the end' — offers that were politely, even gratefully, declined.

'It might be weeks, Mum,' Linda lied.

On the doorstep Rick hugged his mother, and then — impulsively — his father. The older man, surprised to receive any sign of affection beyond the usual handshake — hugged him back.

'Be strong,' he said. 'Our thoughts are with you.'

On the last evening the smaller family ate together at the nearby Pizza Hut, a favourite of the childrens. Unwilling to carry Emma, increasingly frail, past a hundred staring faces, Rick had rung the manager; they were permitted to arrive and eat early, half an hour before opening time. If this approached the dimensions of a Last Wish, it was never mentioned — and if the ride home would be by tumbril, it would at least be a short trip.

At home afterwards the four played Monopoly — both children as engrossed as always, both parents unable to concentrate, but doing their best, buying and selling properties on autopilot. Apart from the care with which the fragile Emma had been set down on a sheepskin rug and soft pillows, they might have been one of the idealised families pictured on the boxes of other board-games stacked in their shelves, sprawled on carpet in family rooms, with a board between them. Reminders of their life together surrounded them: gift books, home videos, souvenirs of family holidays, framed paintings done by the children at school or kindergarten or home, family photographs. If the big open space at the back of the house was more family shrine or chapel than family room, these photographs were its icons: small framed group portraits of the four, a smattering of older ancestors, but above all, everywhere the glowing photographs of Ben and Emma, at various ages.

As the game finished, it occurred to Rick that this room had always been their true place of worship, not Church – and that these three people, his family, his ideal of Family, had always been the core of whatever he believed in.

Later, sitting at his desk in his study, listening to Mozart, he finished a long letter to his parents, asking for forgiveness, hoping for understanding. He also tore open the last letter he had written to Ben, to be read on his eighteenth birthday, and added several more words of love. Perhaps it was the Mozart, perhaps it was the sedative leaching into his veins, but with these tasks completed he found himself facing events if not with equanimity, at least once again with certainty.

Linda appeared in the door, agitated, trembling: 'We can't go through with this. It's absurd.'

He led her into the bedroom, they lay down together on the bed, and held each other tightly. They had planned to make love one last time, but the act suddenly seemed irrelevant, and meaningless. She was still trembling; he rose and fossicked a Bible from the bookshelves, and for a time they read alternately: the poetry of Isaiah, Paul's letters to the Corinthians, St Matthew's version of the Sermon on the Mount, various Psalms. The texts held only a minimal promise for Rick – 'we'll see,' he joked grimly to himself – but some deeper music in the words had a soothing effect on both of them, like the drug he had swallowed, or the Mozart itself: *Yea, though I walk through the valley of the shadow of death, I will fear no evil: for thou art with me* . . .

He might believe in little beyond family love, but these words seemed the culmination of all their nights of book-readings, as if those thick books – Dickens, George Eliot, Thackeray – had been a preparation for this moment, this last distillation of the written word.

In the next room Ben landed on Mayfair, with hotels; the children abandoned their game and joined their parents in bed. Linda slipped a small butterfly-needle into Rick's veins, and taped it in place, despite shaking hands; she then repeated the procedure on Emma, finding the task surprisingly easy: the girl's veins were more prominent than her father's, her skin far more delicate than any thick-skinned navel orange. Emma flinched, momentarily, then watched solemnly as two syringes were loaded with morphine. Her wide owl-eyes seemed to be looking at everything simultaneously, taking everything in. They lay together on the bed, all four of them — just as they had been together at Emma's birth, six years earlier, in the Maternity Suite at the local hospital. Ben seemed finally to grasp the enormity of what was planned, his eyes had reddened, but the seriousness, the methodical ritual of events seemed to keep any terror in check. They had debated allowing him to watch, to participate, but even now, at the point of no return, there was surely something less terrifying, and certainly less bloody, about this occasion for him than there had been at his sister's birth, when her strange alien-being seemed to burst from his mother's innards. Linda felt that for his peace of mind later, as an adult, he should be a participant, he should be there. He listened quietly as they explained the last few steps, he kissed his father, and lay on top of him.

And so they lay together, a last few minutes of hand-holding, and tears, before separating. Emma seemed less concerned than her brother. Her clear contentment, lying there, clutching his hand, forced the last doubts from Rick's mind, and induced a parallel contentment in him. His heart pounded, but the flow of his thoughts was suddenly calm and steady. Even Linda felt that her daughter's serenity somehow cancelled out, at least for the moment, whatever misery she and her surviving child would subsequently endure.

When her husband was ready, she nodded, and pressed her face softly onto his, and he squeezed his own syringe, and waited, holding them all, but not for any length of time.

READING NOTES

AFTERWORD

While much of what I have written becomes unreadable or embarrassing as it recedes into the past, a few things, at least, seem to move in the opposite direction, improving with age. Perhaps this is to meet the requirements of some unknown physical law, a conservation of achievement that requires an average mediocrity. If enough bad writing is written, an equal and opposite amount of good must therefore arise? If so, I should try to write more badly, more often.

Jesus Wants Me For A Sunbeam has passed my personal test of time – so far. One reason a story or poem might avoid disillusioning is that it refuses to have its meanings exhausted by rereading; it will not allow the reader (and the writer is the first reader) to be bored. It continues to yield crops, including some from seeds which weren't consciously sown at the time of writing. I haven't exhausted *Sunbeam* – I still see new things in it.

Today I thought I saw this: the worship of family is a deep and nourishing religious practice. In our secular society, we might pretend to believe in very little – but of course we believe in much, even if we keep our deepest and most sacred beliefs hidden from ourselves. The urge to religious belief is hot-wired into us according to the anthropologist Walter Burkert. In his book, *Creation of the Sacred: Tracks of Biology in Early Religion*, Burkert traces how religious belief takes similar forms (e.g. sacrifice) in different cultures. Like our sexual impulses, our religious beliefs resist the attempts of local culture to suppress them, although cultural pressure always deforms these biological imperatives into interesting and unique local shapes, going by the names of (say) Christianity, or Animism, or Islam, or even High Church Modernism.

I've explored this in a little more detail in two essays – 'The Biology of Literature', and 'Waiting for the Martians' in my collection of essays, *Navel Gazing*.

When other gods fail, there is still the worship of family, and the household gods of this last surviving religion are its children. But what happens when those cute gods fail? Family worship takes many forms – from the sentimental pieties of Hollywood, to the countless automatic rituals and routines that deeply nourish domestic life. In us we trust? The line from a John Berryman poem has always echoed in my head. The

Afterword

sacredness of family is also surely hot-wired into us, if partly for the usual genetically selfish reasons. What blood sacrifices might be offered to that sacred faith? What crimes committed in its name? Me against my brother; my brother and I against our cousins; our cousins and us against the world excuses everything from fratricide through clan warfare to ethnic cleansing and genocide – but there may be more subtle, suburban weirdness to emerge from family worship. This story explores one such little nuclear detonation.

Sunbeam strikes me more and more as a special story; certainly in the sense that it is a story that no-one has written before. It has another claim on me: as a father in love with my children, I understood it instinctively, before I began to half-understand it at a rational level. It seemed, simply, true.

The best stories are often deceptively simple; they speak to us, to our unconscious, in ways that can not be immediately grasped; but we feel the fit, even as we are horrified, or awed.

Stories about the death of children are not new, of course – they are among the oldest, their common tune one of the most easily played for effect. Dickens killed more babies than a minor diphtheria epidemic, and even Oscar Wilde's famous comment that anyone who could read the death of Little Nell without laughing 'had a heart of stone' is surely a defence against his own suppressed sentimentality. Wilde may or may not have convinced himself, but he has helped to convince us: a Dickensian rendering – a rending – of the death of a child is impossible in today's fictional world. 'The blood of the children flowed in the streets . . . like the blood of the children,' Pablo Neruda wrote in a famous attack on the use of artistic effects, such as simile and metaphor, to describe the unspeakable. Tell it plainly, I assume he was saying. Tell it as it is – at least when speaking of real deaths, real events.

But in the world of fiction?

Fiction is a different way of seeing – even its most plain-talking stories operate at a more mythic, universal level. It aims to tell the truth, yes – but in essence, in symbol, in a deeper emotional language that illuminates the particulars.

After Dickens and Wilde – and Hollywood – stories must pluck at our emotions more subtly.

This story has an odd logic – but I hope it is a logic which still locks us in, subtly, and carries us, disbelief suspended, from comforting and loving suburban beginnings into a zone not so much twilight as midnight.

Afterword

Like crabs in slowly heated water, we find ourselves — I hope — being boiled alive, without noticing how we got there.

Where are we?

Among ancient instincts of sacrifice, and the dark comfort that the dying find in taking others with them, if given a chance, in their pyramids, on their funeral pyres, in their Berlin bunkers. In a world of repressed or sublimated spirituality. In a place where the logic of love has carried us further than it had any right to do. Perhaps.

I've added a few pages to the 1993 version which first appeared in the collection *Little Deaths*.

What we write is usually too much or too little — or looks that way later. I usually err too much towards too little. I used to think the story was perfect, of course it wasn't, and still isn't, but it will probably continue to aspire to perfection when it has the chance.

PETER GOLDSWORTHY 1999

Peter Goldsworthy has written a number of poems whose concerns overlap those of the novella *Jesus Wants Me For A Sunbeam*. A reading of these poems might enhance an understanding of the novella.

Songs on the Death of Children

I

Dry eyed after so many deaths
how many could still bring tears?
family and friends
I count on a handful of fingers
and all the children in the world.
With children
the first million is hardest.

II

I walk through their sleeping ward.
Among heads inflated with dreams,
faces loosened on pillows.
Among small milky breaths, smaller than words.
My child
and the children of others.
Shared animal young,
possum eyed and thimble nosed —
shapes that every kind of love recognises.

III

I wake to death
in the night.
The cold weight
of a child in a mother's arms.
Locked from her grief
and the whole archipelago of parents

weeping with her—
the uselessness of tears.
In this public ward
her private room of pain.

IV
I bring my child home
to smiles and somersaults.
Bedtime rhymes
taken after meals
for the treatment.
I watch her by night
dreaming through her fears,
her small milky breath
smaller than tears.

Ratepayer's Ode

*He walks through an afternoon
of sunlight and neighbours.
Along avenues of home loans,
almost paid.*

*Slow flies bump at his face,
webs itch like memories.
The cosmetics of summer surround him—
the detonation of fruit trees,
the shallows of lawn.*

*A paperboy rides towards him
throwing novels into every yard.
He unwraps the headlines and reads.
It is science fiction again.
It is always science fiction.*

The Dark Side of the Head

After a line by Wittgenstein
I.M. Gwen Harwood, 1920–1995

Just around the corner of the eye,
at every reach of its big screen,
there is a magic which is neither
black nor white, but only absent:
the disappearance of all world.

Even when the eyes are shut,
and all the field is pink or dark,
it still unhappens, at the rim
—a sudden gradual nothing,
beneath the notice, or beyond.

I sometimes hope that if
my head jerks leftwards, quick
as warp, I might just catch
the edge of right-side visual field,
as if there is no dark side of the head

but one world only, seamless,
like the small curved universes
painted on Grecian urns,
or like a Mercator projection
of the globe, that having mapped

itself, bent weirdly at the polar
ends, for flat-screen eyes,
now unmaps in reverse, becoming
whole again and full and round
and as satisfactory as heaven.

Eye of the Needle

I.M. Philip Hodgins, 1959–1995

i

*In the earth
there are doorways
from this earth
but they are narrow.*

ii

*the weight of matter
keeps it down to earth,
as if the property called mass
is store-security, a clip-on
tag-alarm that stops us
taking our garment
when we leave the shop.*

iii

*Thoughts are already things
before they're set to ink.
Their heaviness is hard
to measure, but material,
being stuff in the head.
Weigh the brain before
and after thinking,
the difference is no
laughing matter, too real
to follow us through Exits.*

iv
*Even light
is far too heavy.
It must be dark
through there.*

DEATH AND THE COMEDIAN

An essay by Peter Goldsworthy

1.

Tell me your favourite jokes, and I will tell you your worst fears.

I sometimes use that line, across late night dinner tables, when conversation flags. It should not be confused with S.J. Perelman's request: tell me your phobias and I will tell you what you are afraid of — which is, incidentally, one of my favourite jokes.

I once dined with friends at Kinsella's, a Sydney funeral parlour turned restaurant. We were seated in the inner sanctum, the former chapel. Mid-meal, the poet Elizabeth Riddell recalled that her last visit to Kinsella's had been fifteen years before, for a funeral.

Her late husband's coffin, she announced, had occupied the precise spot where our table now stood.

Such ability to look death calmly, even jokily, in the eye, and continue eating, impressed me no end. It also suggested the possibility of finding a narrative tone with which to handle the various stories of death, and grief, and near-death which I had been collecting – or which had been collecting me – for years.

A few weeks before Philip Hodgins death from leukaemia in 1995, I prepared a newspaper obituary after a request from Philip had been passed on through a mutual friend. Philip had finally decided to discontinue the chemotherapy which had caused him much suffering for many years. I sent him the obituary – he was curious to read it – and a few days later received a bottle of his favourite wine, Passing Clouds, accompanied by a congratulatory note: it was 'an obituary to die for.'

This seems to me one of the great aphorisms, deserving of a place in any collection of aphorisms – and a perfect distillation of Philip's stoic courage, and style. It's also a seamless mix of favourite joke and worst fear.

1995 was a bad year for Australian poetry, with the death of Gwen Harwood after a year long battle with what she, also, knew to be a terminal illness. Whatever private demons this forced her to wrestle with, or share with her husband and family, in her letters she remained cheerful and courageous – and as irreverent as ever, her characteristic humour irrepressible.

I can walk (as if on Jupiter) very slowly, I even look like an alien from another planet; moon-faced and swollen from the medications & decorated with magenta blotches. How uninteresting . . .

This from the last letter I was privileged to receive, a few weeks before her death.

It would be nice to think that we could all face our own ends with the same courage, and dignity, and tough humour.

I often thought I was dying as a child, suffering attacks of asthma at harvest time – but I liked to over-dramatise. I did spend a week in intensive care in my early twenties with a chest full of blood – but I was too drugged to sense any danger, or take proper stock. The days passed in a dream, interrupted only by the worried faces of my parents emerging and vanishing through the fog of narcotics.

What, me worry?

My experience of death has (obviously) been from the outside, looking on – but the experience has been all too frequent.

2.

People often ask how I manage to mix working as a writer with working as a doctor. Or – an interesting wording — which are you 'really'. Part of me always resents this: why should the two trades be incompatible, or immiscible? Perhaps the surprise that people express at such a mix — writing and medicine — is due to received notions of an Art/Science Great Divide, notions which are much exaggerated, and usually come as a complete surprise to anyone on the science side of the alleged divide, most of whom read novels, watch movies and listen to music avidly.

Sometimes the question comes from the other side, from an opposite set of prejudices: sometimes it's a logistics question. How can a Busy Doctor Have Time to Write Books? There's a subtext here, an accusation that harks back to that use of the word 'really': the notion that a 'real' doctor would not bother with anything so frivolous.

And another, different part of me sympathises with this. It's a question I often ask myself, as any good Methodist boy would — especially late at night, when the work of Making Up Stories often seems rather silly.

I find it's useful to quote Anton Chekhov in such circumstances, especially to myself: 'medicine is my wife, writing is my mistress.'

Writing is my Golf Afternoon? In fact, I suspect that my temperament is more suited to writing than to medicine. Ever since I treated a fractured right leg in my first year out of medical school by putting a plaster on the left leg I've had a feeling that life held out something else for me beyond medicine. Fortunately no harm was done, except to my ego. I removed the wet plaster, red-faced, and reapplied it to the other side. Creative medicine? Or gross negligence? I blame a wandering mind, a mind too often occupied elsewhere. I like to jot down ideas between patients in a notebook I keep for that purpose. Recently a chemist around the corner returned a prescription to me with the note that while he enjoyed the poem, he didn't think it one of my best.

And here is one of the advantages of writing as a career: you don't need to be particularly alert to succeed. You don't need to know the difference between a right leg and a left leg for instance. Or if you do, then you've got a few weeks or even months to think about it, and make up your mind exactly which is which. If it's about nothing else, writing is about patience.

But if the literary sensibility offers little help in the practice of medicine – and might even prove a hindrance – what of vice versa?

'I don't know a better training for a writer than to

spend some years in the medical profession,' Somerset Maugham, a graduate of the Class of 1897, wrote. Perhaps, perhaps not. Medicine, like any work which involves contact with a lot of human misery — and human stupidity — tends to shrivel the heart. To survive, or at least to sleep peacefully, it quickly becomes essential to put some sort of distance between that world and yourself. I think I was happiest during my student years when working in the Emergency Ward of the hospital in which I trained. Emergency Ward medicine is medicine at its most personally distant, disproportionately removed from the extreme pain and severity of the illnesses and injuries which ambulances disgorge into that ward at all hours of the day and night. It's a world akin to the Mental Arithmetic tests of primary school (I was good at Mental!), a world of inadequate history taking, too-rapid examinations, forced decisions.

I found Emergency far easier to handle, emotionally, than the protracted problems and pains of patients I came to know in other wards, and in general practice since, daily. There is simply insufficient time in Emergency to worry too much about any single person; there is always another stretcher arriving, another set of rapid decisions to be made.

It's a world oddly free of worry; far too busy for the luxury of worry.

I imagine that many medicos have been in the same emotional boat, if only because the selection processes for medical schools favour (or used to favour) applicants who are good at Mental Arithmetic, and not necessarily good at coping with pain, theirs or others.

That doctors often come to see the suffering, or dying, of their patients as an intellectual puzzle to be solved is one way of handling the pressures of such an emotionally overwhelming world.

It's a mind-set easy to caricature: the heartless medical students of *Pickwick Papers*; or Herman Melville's Surgeon-Of-The-Fleet Cadwallader Cuticle come to mind: '*He walked abroad, a curious patchwork of life-and-death, with a wig, one glass eye and a set of false teeth . . . They say he can drop a leg in one minute and ten seconds from the moment the knife touches it.*'

Humour, of course, is another way of maintaining distance: medical school gallows humour. We all, supposedly, remember our first day at school with clarity – psychiatrists lay great store in the emotional content of those childhood recollections. I'm sure that all medicos remember their first day at medical school, which is also their first day in the Dissecting

Room, with even greater clarity. For some that first visit lasts only a few seconds before they bolt for the door; for most curiosity reaches a delicate balance with nausea.

I managed to resist throwing up until I arrived home to face dinner – when some variant of Murphy's Law ensured there would be cold pork on the table, that night of all nights.

Cold short pork.

Organ fights, or flesh fights, were not unknown in the Dissecting Room – although such irreverence was harshly dealt with by the authorities. I clearly remember being hit on the head by a stray human testicle one sun-drenched afternoon. It's not the kind of event you easily forget.

Richard Gordon ('Doctor in the House' etc.) made a fortune out of books filled with such undergraduate pranks – but it's the opposite defence against the unspeakable that is perhaps more interesting to a writer; the defence of coldness, of denial. Over a period of years, working long hours, and with no sabbaticals to allow a refilling of the reservoirs of compassion, the gallows-humour process in many doctors goes too far, and becomes its own caricature: cynicism, indifference.

I've often parodied that too-clinical voice in my own writing – in part such self-parodies are an exorcism, or an attempted exorcism, although this is not always the way reviewers see it. This, from a review of one of my books by Andrea Stretton in the *Sydney Morning Herald*:

This sparse and understated prose brings out this reader's bloodlust: the desire for one of these fictional medicos to undergo major fictional surgery – without an anaesthetic.

A little more favourable, from *The Weekend Australian*:

His style has an initial bedside manner before slitting open a dark underbelly of irony.

Most memorable is this, from a review by Brian Matthews in *The Adelaide Review*:

Ask not for whom the bleeper bleeps, it bleeps for thee.

I find all this use of medical metaphor mildly irritating. But its probably better to be a doctor reviewed by writers, than a writer reviewed by doctors. This is what happened to Jonathon Swift's *Gulliver's Travels* when it was discussed in an issue of the *Psychoanalytic Quarterly*:

Jonathon Swift showed marked anal characteristics (extreme personal immaculateness, secretiveness, intense ambition, pleasure in less obvious dirt, stubborn vengefulness in righteous causes) which indicate that early control of his excretory function was achieved under great stress and perhaps too early.

3.

If we remember our first day in the dissecting room clearly, we also remember our first day in labour ward. Being present at childbirth is to share in a huge joy — there is so much joy to go around, a little spills over into all but the most jaded heart. It is always, as if for the first time, to experience a thrilling shock — for there is something shocking, and dislocating, in the final emergence of that new small slippery being.

The image in the film *Alien*, as the pupal-stage alien bursts from the chest of the host human, captures some of the weird other-worldly shock of the first childbirth I ever saw.

Paradoxically, as a doctor, I find my greatest satisfaction now comes from the treatment of, or more accurately the offering of assistance to, the dying. Satisfaction may seem an odd word for this work, which is often emotionally harrowing — but its satisfactions *are* deeply nourishing. Palliative care, in the argot, has recently, and not before time, become a growth specialty. Being present at death — death at home, among loved ones, from which pain has been banished, and in which the dying person has been granted time and space to come to terms with the fact — to be part of this, in however small and peripheral a way, is a huge and humbling privilege. To write about it is near-impossible: firstly, to decide if you have the right, secondly, to tread the fine line between mawkish sentimentality, and too-clinical distance.

Several times I've used a female doctor persona to represent the 'feminine' side of these feelings: the caring side. Its opposite, the objective 'masculine' practitioner, has variously been transformed into a pedantic Latin scholar, and, more recently, a mathematician, obsessed by that purest of the sciences, a world free from any human contamination.

In part such representations are another exorcism, and no doubt somewhere between the two is an ideal narrator: a narrator who can handle all the stories of horror, squalor, stupidity, death – and occasional transcendent courage, or love – for which I can't yet find a proper focus, or tone.

Of course, death is not easily house-trained; it is rarely so amenable to human management and control – to the schedules of an idealised Good Death. It's more often sudden, or violent, or cruel, or painful, or terrifying.

And its world, and the stories from that world, are almost unfathomable.

A mother injects her baby with poison, repeatedly, to gain it admission to hospital. As soon as the baby is separated from the mother, it improves – back in her care, it deteriorates. She denies everything, and almost certainly believes herself.

A doctor saves a choking friend's life in a restaurant, and the saved friend cannot bring himself to speak to his saviour again – the debt is too great to acknowledge, or even admit.

A woman brings in photographs 'of my accident' – photographs of herself, a seriously injured road victim, being extracted from wreckage, bandaged, loaded into an ambulance. The inevitable question is asked: 'Who took the photographs?' The answer: 'Oh, my husband took the photographs.'

My husband, the amateur *paparazzo*.

What to make of these true, baffling stories? I'm not even sure that they are my business. They do provide a different scale of priorities of importance; an idea of what is, finally, 'really' important, to borrow back that same criterion I tossed up earlier in this piece.

And perhaps this is part of the reason I cannot get enthusiastic about much of the highly-praised writing in this country – and others – in recent years. So much of it belongs in those underrated literary categories: Plain Silly, or Dead Boring.

Including most of my own. For these are the categories of the puritan, of course: the Methodist boy in me who I have also attempted to caricature, but seem unable to shake off entirely. Too many years of medical training, perhaps, have cemented it permanently in place. If part of me likes to see itself as an upper-case Writer – a narcissocrat, a junior member of the priest caste of our silly Art-worshipping culture – another part is always accusing: Fine, But What Are You Going To Do When You Grow Up?

And yet turning these stories into fiction might help towards some kind of understanding, towards finding some essence, beyond curiosity, or voyeurism. Fiction is above all a re-ordering process, a sense-making process, even when it's black comedy. Jokes, too, are a form of fiction; albeit a particularly poetic form. 'Undoubtedly the world is, and her riches can never be circumscribed by art' the Polish poet Czeslaw Milosz has written – but we have to make a start, especially under immense pressure from the emotions that surround death. Sometimes, to use an old truism, if we don't laugh, we cry – and sometimes even both at the same time, our worst jokes and favourite fears tangled hopelessly together.

PETER GOLDSWORTHY 1993

When *Jesus Wants Me For A Sunbeam* was first released in the collection *Little Deaths* in 1993 it received considerable acclaim and attention. Following are a number of reviews that discuss the power and importance of the novella.

REVIEWS

'Death in the suburbs mirrored in irony'
ANDREW RIEMER, *Sydney Morning Herald, 1993*

Peter Goldsworthy is probably the most stylish of our writers. His work is distinguished by elegance, by sharpness of observations, by nicely judged ironies and by memorable, aphoristic turns of phrase. He is a most careful craftsman, who hones and polishes his work, paying close attention to nuances and implications.

. . . Goldsworthy shows wonderful control of tone and implication. These pieces [in *Little Deaths*] are, without exception, marvellously shaped, often wry epiphanies. Most of them capture moments where the characters must face a bleak future, without hope of consolation. Yet such is the tightly controlled and allusive nature of these stories that we do not, as a rule, catch the character in the grip of suffering or rage.

Goldsworthy seems to draw back from the representation of passion or states of extreme emotion. And that, or so it seems to me, is a limitation to these fine, highly civilised stories.

. . . *Jesus Wants Me For A Sunbeam* [is] a *tour de force* of control and compression. Rick and Linda seem blessed with everything fortune can bestow. They are intelligent, cultivated, socially responsible people who approach their duty as the parents of two young children with level-headed seriousness. They seem to stand therefore, as shining emblems of all that is admirable about moderate and well-considered lives – a guarantee, perhaps, of the moral strengths of humanism.

Their life is nevertheless shattered when one of the children contracts an incurable disease. One of the many fine things in this splendid novella is Goldsworthy's meticulous description – based no doubt on his experiences as a medical practitioner – of the progress of the disease and the fluctuating reactions of those obliged to stand helplessly by. At the end, Linda and Rick are forced to face the implications of death more directly and with more surprising consequences than usual in these stories or in Goldsworthy's work in general.

When we reach the end of this disturbingly memorable tale, Goldsworthy obliges us to acknowledge something that is latent and expertly implied in the earlier sections. Linda and Rick, those exemplars of the most admirable facets of our world, people keenly aware of the degrading effects of violence and brutality in our everyday experience, are defenceless against the fact of death — especially the death of a child. The most painful recognition this remarkable story brings home is that a sanely secular world crumbles in the face of such a fact.

And all this, I must add, is accomplished in 45 pages. The feat is admirable, yet even here I am conscious of a certain holding-back, perhaps reticence. Why didn't Goldsworthy let go and write the big, even chaotic novel hiding inside this "little death"?

'Life and death near and afar'
KATHARINE ENGLAND, *The Advertiser, Adelaide, 1993*

Goldsworthy's talent is for the local and particular — each story a polished miniature, an acid-etched Adelaide gem. His scene-setting is minimal: his characters — clones of our intelligent, hard-working, right-minded selves — fill the page, seeming first to have followed the doctor's traditional injunction: go behind the screen and take off your clothes.

With scalpel-edged prose, Goldsworthy turns back the well-toned tissue, cutting down to a point at which the middle-class gods — education, good manners, real estate, friends, religion, the arts and a healthy, if hard-won, bank account — fail to offer salvation: to the peeled, unsuspected deep point at which something more primitive and wild takes over.

. . . The heart of the collection [*Little Deaths*] details another kind of 'little death', the death of a child, in a novella with the searing title *Jesus Wants Me For A Sunbeam* and the epigraph 'In us we trust'. Goldsworthy describes at length, in a tone that is enigmatic rather than dispassionate, the development of an inward-looking, emotionally self-sufficient little family and their response to the disease which is claiming their six-year-old daughter. This is automatically heart-string-twanging territory, with little scope for wit and the cutting edge: without this balance Goldsworthy's candid simplicity tends to the maudlin – in the context of a longer story his characters are less well-defined, and the weight of the story is carried uneasily by its emotive subject matter, by every parent's superstitious, sympathetic fear.

'Death of a middle-class lady'
PETER O'CONNOR, *The Age, 1994*

... [In *Little Deaths*] Goldsworthy magnifies the issues of life and our feeble and pointless attempts to construct order and the illusion of certitude against the inevitability of death itself. It is by exploring the presence of death that the author forces the reader into reflecting upon the transitory nature of life with death as the only certainty.

This is not to suggest that his stories are morbid, serious and depressing. In fact, his genius as a writer is that he engages us in a whole range of emotions from humour and farce to profound sadness, each time holding a kaleidoscope up to the existence of death, allowing us to look at it and reflect upon it from many different angles. However, the result is always the same: the inevitability of death against the transitoriness of life.

... It is the novella [*Jesus Wants Me For A Sunbeam*] that stands out as the centrepiece of this collection. In this story, he skilfully explores the feelings of an ordered and symmetrical couple who have planned all their life down to their one of each gender child, only to suddenly discover that one of the children is suffering from the incurable disease of leukaemia.

The exposition of the gradual breakdown in belief systems, the utter futility of the Christian response and the final stark and brutal solution of a father committing suicide in order to reassure the child that he will be waiting for her after her death, is simply brilliant and utterly engaging.

In this story and throughout the collection [*Little Deaths*], Peter Goldsworthy writes with a sort of underlying expectancy of uncertainty, daring the reader to stretch their known boundaries and explore with him unknown and desolate areas of the psyche, including the great unknown, death itself. His masterfully crafted volume challenges us to explore death in a way that leaves one compelled to reflect upon life and the futility of the fantasy of permanence, regardless of what means we use to construct that fantasy.

'Death sentences'

PHILIP HODGINS, *The Sydney Review, 1993*

In these stories, as in all Goldsworthy's fiction, the prose is spare, polished and nervy. He understands that fundamental thing about writing fiction: people like stories. He's a great exemplar of the fact that when you simply get on with the job of telling a story the narrative action creates character, atmosphere, suspense, interest, etc. And that if you do you won't have to waste the reader's time joining up the dots and colouring in the spaces. Instead, he has the skill to come in just every now and then with a single revealing detail that fills out the canvas satisfyingly.

. . . The novella that follows these stories, *Jesus Wants Me For A Sunbeam*, is the emotional core of this collection. A young couple who have two children are presented with a stunning death sentence: one of their children has a terminal disease.

Like most parents, they had rehearsed over the years for that moment, emotionally: the moment they might hear the work leukaemia spoken to them, spoken at them. They had grieved, vicariously, for other children: small strangers who were nevertheless part of the shared public property of parenthood. News of the illnesses of these others — friends of cousins of friends, or cousins of friends of cousins — spread as rapidly as jokes or gossip through a vast network of waiting, eaves-dropping parents, in hushed, horrified tones.

The bizarre events that follow are typical of the way Goldsworthy denies expectation. In this case the denouement is even more extreme than might have been imagined, and the reader is left with a lingering, troubling sadness; the sort of sadness Goldsworthy explored in his early poems 'Gustave Mahler: Kindertotenlieder' and 'Songs on the Death of Children'.

. . . For Goldsworthy is above all else a poet. The stories and novella in this collection, as well as the poem itself, show a poet's talent for concision and the poet's ability to notice telling details.

ABOUT PETER GOLDSWORTHY

Peter Goldsworthy was born in Minlaton, South Australia, in 1951, and grew up in various country towns in which his father was a teacher, and later, a high school headmaster. His mother also trained as a teacher.

In a 1996 essay 'A Country Childhood', Goldsworthy described his earliest memories of country landscapes and activities, and childhood illness. *'I loved to ride the tractor in the harvesting season but I never lasted in the driver's seat for long. My nose would run, then I would start wheezing. The local doctor, Paddy Reilly, liked to sit on my sickbed and reassure me. "Don't worry lad, nobody ever died of asthma." This dangerous lie at least had a calming effect – and of course he didn't have much else to offer besides comforting lies. These were the days before inhalers and nebulisers.'*

Goldsworthy finished his schooling in Darwin, the setting for his widely acclaimed novel *Maestro*. *'Dostoevsky says that the best education for a writer is a single glowing memory from childhood. The moment of illumination in my case might be my arrival at Darwin airport at two am on a wet season morning in 1966. The air was hot and humid. The scents that enveloped us as we walked towards the unimpressive terminal overpowered even the fumes of aviation fuel that make most airports indistinguishable. The smell of Darwin was a mix of tropical fecundity and rot — a sweet and sour compost smell. It has a climate that tires humans but encourages all kinds of insect and botanic life.'*

Darwin saw the beginning of Goldsworthy's dual career as a writer and doctor, with a little help from his father. *'At school I was good at sport and shone at maths and science. I was set to be a zoologist or maybe a physicist. Then two things happened which changed the priorities in my life. A friend and I started a club called The Freethinkers — I began to read for the first time the books that my dad had given me years before. The other new development was that I lost interest in maths. I shared a desk with a girl in the back row and we preferred to explore other areas of knowledge than matrices and probability theory. When exams were a few months away, my father realised I was going to fail maths and therefore would not be able to pursue the career of my choice. He crossed the boundary between school and home and commandeered my evenings and weekends. My friends went hooning around, I stayed indoors with the calculus textbook learning integration by the only way that delivers results – solving a thousand problems. I passed well enough to get into medicine and became a doctor. I have my father to thank for not giving up on me and for retaining some influence over me at a time when I was victimising the other teachers and generally being obnoxious.'*

Goldsworthy went on to graduate in medicine from the University of Adelaide and has devoted his time since equally to medicine and writing. He married a fellow graduate, and has three children. He has published three collections of poetry, including *This Goes With That: Selected Poems 1970–1990*, and four collections of short fiction, including *Little Deaths*. He is the author of four novels: *Maestro*, *Honk If You Are Jesus*, *Wish*, *Keep It Simple, Stupid*, and a novel written jointly with Brian Matthews, *Magpie*. He has won numerous awards including the Commonwealth Poetry prize and an Australian Bicentennial Literary Award. His novels have been translated into many Asian and European languages.

Goldsworthy doesn't believe medicine and writing are as disparate as some people feel. His medical life provides a privileged exposure to people that he draws on extensively for his writing. *'I think medicine teaches us to observe people in some extent, which is probably good for novelists – part of the art of diagnosis is observation.'*

These days Goldsworthy feels more at home in the city than the countryside of his childhood. Again from 'A Country Childhood': *'Fourteen years after we left Minlaton, I revisited for the first time. I ended up in the local hospital with a severe asthma attack. It's as though I'm allergic to my roots.'* Despite this Goldsworthy still believes that a country childhood has its benefits, *'The city suits me now and the bush has changed. It's probably still the best place for kids though. The best place to acquire a nose for bullshit, to learn how this country came to be what it is, and to learn the basic connections — that milk comes from cows, meat from animals, canes from canefields. There are more miracles out there per hectare, and enough room for all kinds of childhood creativity.'*

DISCUSSION QUESTIONS

Following are a number of possible discussion points for reading groups or school groups:

1) *'Of course we have to concede that all literature is reductionist in essence — it seeks to capture and to simplify a world that is rich and varied beyond the scope of language. Any description is, necessarily, a simplification.' Peter Goldsworthy.*
Goldsworthy has often said that he is interested in the 'precision' and 'perfection' of storytelling. Do you see these qualities in Jesus Wants Me For A Sunbeam?

2) *The notions of balance and harmony appear frequently in* Jesus Wants Me For A Sunbeam. *Would you agree? What do you see as their significance — as both thematic and stylistic devices?*

3) *Goldsworthy's prose has been described as 'scalpel-edged', 'clinical' and 'tightly controlled'. He has been criticised for not showing his character's emotions more and not imbuing his prose with enough 'warmth' and 'empathy'. Is this apparent lack of emotion and compassion a justified criticism of* Jesus Wants Me For A Sunbeam?

4) *In the novella Rick and Linda lead very sheltered, protected lives, isolating themselves from the troubles of the world. Would you say the novella criticises this lifestyle, because through Emma's illness Rick and Linda are forced to confront the tragedy of the world they have sought to avoid?*

5) *What does the novella say about the relationship between parent and child, and the 'responsibility' implied within that relationship?*

6) *Peter Goldsworthy is also well-known for his poetry and many critics consider his prose to be poetic. What do you find poetic about* Jesus Wants

Discussion Questions

Me For A Sunbeam? What similarities and differences do you see between Peter Goldsworthy's poetry, such as 'Songs on the Death of Children' and the novella itself?

7) *What role does Reason play within the text? Are the final decisions 'reasonable'?*

8) *How strong is the sense of family within the novella? What does the novella mean by its depiction of the 'shrine' of the family?*

9) *What does the novella say about the power of books? Do the books of Rick and Linda — Dickens, Austen etc — fail them? Or does the novella offer a glimpse of 'the word and its powerful role in Western civilisation'?*

10) *Some readers consider the denouement of* Jesus Wants Me For A Sunbeam *to be 'extreme', an exposure and contemplation of social taboos. What do you see as taboo in the story? How does Goldsworthy present this transgression?*

11) *In what ways do Rick and Linda represent a particularly baby-boomer attitude to and/or awareness of themselves and others? Is their attitude to their children different to that of their parents'?*

12) *It has been suggested that the novella presents the breakdown of the Christian belief system in the face of death. Do you see the story as challenging issues of spirituality — with the failure of the Church to address the young couple's needs and the emergence of their own beliefs?*

13) *'Novels, I decided, were little more than a patchwork quilt of poems and short stories and character sketches and fragments from the writer's notebook, sewn loosely together into what was — after all — a marketable commodity. The poem seems a more natural literary form, as old as song. The short story likewise: as old as the joke, or the campfire yarn. But the novel was surely unnatural, an invention of publishers.' Peter Goldsworthy.*
What qualities in Jesus Wants Me For A Sunbeam

do you see that resemble a novel? Or a short story? or a poem? In what ways does it distinguish itself from these narrative forms?

0402.30217